THE

WHEELMAN

THE
WHEELMAN

DUANE
SWIERCZYNSKI

ST. MARTIN'S MINOTAUR

NEW YORK

www.minotaurbooks.com

Library of Congress Cataloging-in-Publication Data

Swierczynski, Duane.
   The wheelman / Duane Swierczynski.—1st ed.
     p. cm.
   ISBN 0-312-34377-9
   EAN 978-0-312-34377-4
   1. Robbery—Fiction. 2. Betrayal—Fiction. 3. Mute persons—Fiction. 4. Organized crime—Fiction. 5. Irish Americans—Fiction. 6. Philadelphia (Pa.)—Fiction. I. Title.

PS3619.W53W47 2005
813'.6—dc22

2005046512

First Edition: October 2005

10 9 8 7 6 5 4 3 2 1

For **M.A., P.L.,** and **S.E.**—my family

FRIDAY
a.m.

I didn't reform, I lost my nerve. I still think it's sensible to want money and if you want money it has to be sensible to go where they have it and make them give you some.

—AL NUSSBAUM

*L*ENNON WATCHED PEOPLE MAKING THEIR WAY UP AND *down Seventeenth Street as the brisk March air whipped around the buildings. Had he been a smoker, Lennon would have savored the last few puffs before pressing the window button and flipping out the butt. Just one cigarette—something for the geeks in khaki pants and navy blue windbreakers to pick up with tweezers, drop into a thick Ziploc bag, tag, log, then store in their evidence cases.*

Maybe someone would get around to analyzing the brand, try to pluck some DNA from the butt.

Part of Lennon would live forever, somewhere, tucked away in the case files of the Federal Bureau of Investigation.

But Lennon didn't smoke. He fiddled with the car radio a bit and watched strangers make their way to various duties and diversions. He used to wonder what motivated them—what made them get up every morning, brush their teeth, shower, eat breakfast, kiss a loved one and possibly a child good-bye. That wasn't for him, and that's probably why Lennon enjoyed these last moments before a big job. It put everything into perspective. You could either be outside, burning shoe leather, reporting to a cubicle, thinking about a report, whatever. Or you could be inside a car, waiting for your accomplices.

Then the alarm went off, and everything went to hell.

Bang

Bang

Bang

HOLDEN WAS RIGHT UP BLING'S ASS. NO NO *NO* YOU ID-
iot. Hang back. Hang *two steps* back.

But it was too late. The big glass door behind Holden swung shut before Bling had a chance to push open the door in front of him. The hidden ACU—the gunpowder-sniffing gizmo—kicked in. Or maybe someone inside tripped it. Didn't matter. Both Bling and Holden were sealed inside the bank vestibule. Even from twenty yards away you could read the expression on Bling's face as his pistol hand smacked against glass: *Motherfuck.* Trapped, like two gerbils in a Habitrail.

Lennon slid the gearshift into drive, checked the rearview and side mirrors, then punched the car forward and to the left, blocking traffic on Seventeenth Street. He turned around. The strong late March sunshine blazed off the bank's white stone so fiercely it hurt the eyes. Lennon still had a choice. He could leave them behind. Holden deserved it. Bling was another story. And this whole job was another story still.

Lennon pressed two fingers to his neck, feeling for his carotid artery. He counted quickly.

Everything was normal. His pulse hadn't jumped much.

Good.

Hooking an arm around the seat, Lennon looked back at Bling.

He was watching Lennon very carefully. Lennon gave him the universal "move to the left" sign with his hand. Bling grabbed a hunk of Holden's windbreaker and yanked him out of the way.

Cars honked and Lennon hammered the gas pedal. He would have given them the finger, but there wasn't time.

In the rearview, the bank came rushing forward like the view from a cockpit in a plane barreling into the ground. Lennon made tiny adjustments, keeping his gloved hands light on the wheel. A nudge to the left, a tap to the right. He had to hit the glass just right.

He had done enough reading to know that ACUs—access-control-units—were designed to be bulletproof from the inside. That way, the bank nabs a crew of stupid Holden-like bad guys, they can't go whipping out their Sig Sauers and blasting their way out. Banks don't like customers getting popped. They do everything in their power to avoid it. In fact, when they first started making ACUs, they forgot to make them bulletproof, and banks got shot to hell when freaked-out heisters panicked. Some models of ACUs even have these little escape holes, so the heisters can go on their merry way without plugging any of the customers.

Not this model, though. This apparently was the Scratch-Your-Nuts-Until-the-Feds-Arrive™ model. Bulletproof inside and, most likely, out.

But car-proof? Speeding car-proof? Speeding, stolen-Acura-proof?

At the last minute, Lennon saw that he was going to smack into a metal support column. He cut it hard, then felt the glass panes shatter.

He shifted up and tapped forward. Bling grabbed Holden's windbreaker again and pulled him through the gap.

Lennon reached down and popped the back trunk, then checked his watch. 9:13 A.M. They were still on track. As long as they could make the next couple of blocks, this might work out after all. The Acura rocked on its suspension as Bling climbed in shotgun and again as Holden hit the backseat.

Lennon stomped on the gas. The car rocketed forward, tires screaming on pavement, and Lennon didn't see her until the last minute.

The woman, pushing a blue baby stroller.

$650

Large

CENTER CITY PHILADELPHIA BANKS ARE NOT HIT BY takeover teams very often, and with good reason: there are very few ways out.

You get a lot of lone-wolf crackheads doing business, but not many pros. Billy Penn designed Philadelphia to be a tightly locked grid of streets named after trees stretching from the Delaware River to the Schuylkill River. Colonial homes gave way to brownstone mansions which gave way to tightly packed office towers which gave way to a glut of office space. The streets are narrow and often blocked, especially where they lead to interstates. If you are smack-dab in the center of Center City—which Lennon's team was—Interstates 95 and 76 are barely five minutes away. But it can take fifty minutes to reach them, if traffic is shitty enough.

Bling gave Lennon the background. Bling was a Philly boy; Lennon was not. Lennon owned a place deep in the Pocono Mountains just an hour and a half away, and he had people he knew in Philadelphia, but he would never work there. The closest he'd work was New York, and even that was a bit too close.

However, the bankroll was running thin, and Lennon and Katie were finished rolling off a nice long wasted winter, with no work for either of them. It was a nice winter: mostly cooking and reading and drinking. When Bling called Katie in late February, it was the right time to go back to work.

The setup sounded nice, too. Bling needed a wheelman for a three-man takeover. A Wachovia Bank, three blocks from city hall, was set to receive a fat shipment of cash on March 29, straight from the federal government. It was part of the mayor's "Operation Fresh Start," a scheme where he was planning to dump over $650,000 on the shittiest ten-block area in the shittiest part of town, just to level it flat and hope that a national developer would want to build a Barnes & Noble or Bed, Bath & Beyond in the middle of the drug-addled badlands. Most of the money was going to pay one hundred or so holdouts who wanted to stay in their crumbling row houses. Bling told Katie that the mayor was going to hand out between $40,000 and $80,000 to each holdout—in cash—in exchange for surrendering the property.

Why cash? Mayor comes from that area, Bling said. Folks there don't trust nothing but cash. They want to get *paid*. Plus, somebody in the mayor's office thought it would be a good visual for the TV crews: the mayor, launching "Operation Fresh Start" by handing out thick stacks of green to the neediest people in the city. Never mind that gangbangers would probably pounce on the recipients the moment the cameras were turned off. That wasn't the city's problem.

Plus, Bling planned to take the money first.

Bling had a city council snitch who told him about the cash. Bling then told Katie how he planned to pull the thing off, and it sounded like a good idea. So Lennon decided to go back to work.

Certain
Death

L ENNON WAS A VERY GOOD WHEELMAN. STARTING OUT, he was lucky, but then experience and real skill kicked in, and eventually, he earned a reputation.

The moment Lennon saw the woman and her baby stroller, he knew the Acura was going to hit them.

Impact was two or three seconds away. Lennon was faced with a choice: aim for the stroller, or aim for the woman. The woman had at least a slim chance of possessing catlike reflexes and leaping the hell out of the way. Based on an ultraquick glance, she seemed agile enough. Maybe she'd been a state champion gymnast as a teenager.

Braking and wrestling with the wheel was out of the question. The risk of fishtailing was too great, and Lennon worried that he would broadside both the lady and the stroller. Steering clear out of the way was impossible. Immediately to the right of the woman and stroller was one of those huge cement planter squares full of mulch and shrubs. The planter would total the Acura, and the team would have to escape on foot—if any of them were conscious enough to do so. And the car was pointed too far right to be suddenly wrenched to the left. No, the choice was still this: woman or stroller.

"*Fuck!*"

Holden. He had just returned to his originally scheduled programming.

Lennon's hands floated to the right, and his foot tapped the brakes to ease the impact.

The Acura smacked into the woman cleanly, powerfully, directly below her left hip. The impact folded her in half, then sent her tumbling up the windshield and over the hood. Lennon looked in his side-view mirror, and saw—miraculously—the baby stroller, trembling slightly, but still upright on the sidewalk. She had let go, just in time.

Lennon blessed her, even as she skidded off the side of the roof and fell into the street. It was one less thing to explain to Katie.

Passersby screamed, but that wasn't Lennon's concern. Yes, he hoped the woman was still breathing. He hoped her hospital time would be minimal, and that, eventually, she'd forget all about what had happened to her. But he couldn't get caught up in that now. He still had work to do.

The heist had been all on Bling. The getaway was all on him.

The Kennedy Assignation

FOR A GOOD TWO WEEKS, LENNON HAD STUDIED THE street maps of Philadelphia that Bling mailed him, looking for elements that other heisters had overlooked. For the first couple of days, he kept coming back to JFK Boulevard, just one block from the target bank. JFK didn't exist thirty years ago; a huge set of train tracks—nicknamed the "Chinese Wall"—used to cover the same ground, originating from a huge terminal a few blocks to the east. The city shitcanned the trains, then built a row of office complexes and apartment buildings in its wake. They named the street after the recently assassinated U.S. president. *JFK.* Lennon kept coming back to it. It felt right. It felt like the gang's ticket out of the city, out to I-76 and by extension, freedom.

The more Lennon studied, the more he fell in love with JFK. It was a fat street, unlike almost any other in Center City Philadelphia. He took a Martz bus down to study it in person one unseasonably warm day—a Tuesday. His suspicions were confirmed. Even though JFK ran from city hall right to Thirtieth Street Station—arguably the busiest strip of the city—it was wide enough to handle all manner of traffic. Cabbies were able to weave in and out of traffic from Fifteenth Street clear through to Thirtieth. JFK was it: the fat artery that would let the blood spurt away from the heart and straight to I-76.

The only problem: Bling's target bank sat at the corner of Seventeenth and Market. Lennon discovered that Seventeenth Street ran south, *away* from JFK. And Market ran east, *away* from I-76.

He studied the maps, drank imported beer, watched DVD movies with Katie. He knew the answer would come.

It did.

The morning of the job, Bling and Lennon put on window-cleaners' uniforms, then carried their signs and ladders and wooden horses and ropes out of a rented van with the word JENKINTOWN WINDOW MASTERS, INC. painted on the side. (Bling said that all of the decent window-washing companies were based in Jenkintown, a suburb just north of the city.) They set up their gear along the west side of Seventeenth Street, between Market and JFK, arranging the wooden horses in a straight line almost to the end of the curb so that pedestrians would have to walk around them to get anywhere. Chances were, nobody would bother looking up for scaffolding. Besides, it would only have to work for about twenty minutes.

When they had blocked off enough of the sidewalk, Bling and Lennon climbed back into the van, then Bling changed into his second set of clothes—baggy jeans, Vans, oversized basketball jersey. Holden, driving the van, was already dressed for the job. He was wearing an Allen Iverson jersey. Big bright colors, huge fat numbers and names. You want to give them something to look at. That way, they'll keep looking for it later, long after you've changed into something else. Lennon stayed in his window-cleaner uniform. It didn't really matter what he was wearing, not until later.

Bling pulled out his cloned cell phone, dialed in the bomb threat to the U.S. Mint—clear across town—and Lennon drove them to where he'd stashed the Acura.

Easy
Breakage

LENNON WRESTLED THE WHEEL TO THE LEFT AND AP-plied pressure to the brake pedal. The Acura spun forty-five degrees, give or take a degree, so that it faced the wrong way on Seventeenth Street.

"Jesus *fuck* yo!" yelled Holden in the back.

"Hey," said Bling. "Brother knows what he's doin'."

Brother knew *exactly* what he was doing. He just didn't know *how* he was going to do it. The trick was shooting across Market Street in one piece. Lennon knew he had a fifty-fifty shot at a green light, which would make everything easy. A red light would be tricky.

Predictably, the light was red.

Lennon rationalized it. Only sixty feet across. Just sixty measly feet of *Frogger*. Lennon looked back at Bling and nodded, then turned back and pushed down on the accelerator. The Acura jumped forward and raced through the first thirty feet. An SUV tried to cut him off from the last thirty, but Lennon swerved to the left, then cut back to the right and sailed through a parking meter and the traffic pole, directly onto the sidewalk, smashing through the first wooden horse they'd set up. He crashed the Acura through the rest of the window-washing gear—which had been loosened to ensure easy breakage—clear through to JFK Boulevard. Better the gear than innocent people. One hit-and-run victim was enough for one morning.

"Now *that's* how you do it," Bling said.

Lennon shot him a glance in the rearview, then spun left onto JFK and raced forward all the way up to Twentieth Street, weaving in and out of cabs and Mercedes and Chevy Cavaliers. He pressed two fingers to his neck, feeling for the carotid artery. This was his favorite way to gauge stress. He was doing okay, all things considered.

Another rearview check: no flashers. Five blocks away from the bank and nothing. The first five blocks were always the hardest. Lennon took a hard right onto Twentieth Street, going north, then a quick left down a tiny side street that ran parallel to JFK.

Now here's where Philadelphia geography gets interesting. Even after ripping out the Chinese Wall, some bits of the old city remained. Tiny streets and alleys that used to run through the in-dustrial blocks sat right next to the new thoroughfares. One of those alleys was the key to the getaway plan.

The alley Lennon took was wide enough for a car, and led downhill. Right next to it, JFK continued at a level elevation and then turned into a small bridge that ran over the Schuylkill River and directly to the front doors of Thirtieth Street Station. This side alley dipped down to river level. Nobody ever drove on this tiny street.

No sirens yet. Anywhere. A good sign.

The Acura sailed down the side street, crossed Twenty-first Street, then continued to Twenty-second. Lennon made a quick right, then a quick left, and pulled into the parking lot. By this time, Bling and Holden had stripped out of their jerseys and windbreakers and shiny pants and tucked them, along with their guns, into an oversized plastic shopping bag. All Lennon had to do was slip off the window-cleaning uniform, which he handed back to Bling, who tucked it away.

The lot was a park-it-yourself deal. They pulled into a spot, gathered up everything out of the car, then walked over to the second car: a 1998 Honda Prelude. They tucked the plastic bag with their clothes in the trunk next to the canvas bag with the $650,000, tossed the keys in, and slammed the lid shut. Then they calmly walked back to Twenty-second Street to the third car—a Subaru Forester—which was parked on the street. There were still fifteen minutes left on the meter.

Lennon took the keys from his inner suit jacket pocket and pressed the orange button. The security system disengaged with a loud *thew-WEEP WEEP*. He pressed the blue button, and the locks popped. They climbed in, just three business guys carpooling to a meeting in the city.

Except they weren't headed for the city. The gang was headed for Philadelphia International Airport, where they'd take separate flights to different resort hotels in various parts of the world. Holden was headed for a place in Amsterdam. Bling was looking forward to some time on the Left Coast—Seattle. And Lennon was headed for Puerto Rico, to the El Conquistador Hotel and Casino and to Katie, who would be waiting there for him. The $650,000 would stay parked in the trunk of the Prelude. It was a long-term parking lot.

In the first meeting, Holden had had a problem with that part of the caper. "You mean we're going to let it just sit there? What if someone boosts the car?"

"Someone boosts that shit," Bling said, "that's fate. We move on."

"You got to be fucking kidding me."

"It's the safest thing. Trust me—you don't want to be caught with one buck from Wachovia on you. You get nabbed, they ain't got nothing."

"Shit," Holden said. "Someone's gonna boost it."

"Nobody's going to boost it."

Hopefully, nobody was going to boost it.

Lennon pulled the Forester out onto the street, drove up to the parkway, then hooked a right around the art museum and caught Kelly Drive. He had spent a lot of time mapping out this part of the getaway. Lights—only three between the art museum and I-76—were timed; curves studied; proper m.p.h. noted. This was the tiny bit of science involved in Lennon's job. After a few trial runs, Lennon knew that when the light at Fairmount Avenue and Kelly Drive flicked green, he had three seconds to achieve a speed of 38 m.p.h., which would take him to the I-76 entrance without interruption. Lennon was impressed with the city planners; they had obviously taken time to craft this roadway. On some roads, he had to slow down/speed up for particular stretches. Not Kelly Drive. Lennon practically fell in love.

Past the art museum, past Boathouse Row, then deep into Kelly Drive, Lennon finally felt his stomach muscles unclench. The needle of the Subaru was firmly pointed at 38. The rest of the getaway was academic. There was nothing in the car to incriminate them; there were no obstacles between their car and the interstate out of town to the airport.

Lennon smoothly took a curve, looking at the geese assembled by the side of the river. They'd been here a few weeks before, when he'd been scouting the job. A few of them honked. *Goozles.* That's what Katie called them. Something from her childhood. The goozles honked and suddenly fluttered their wings in near-panic.

And that's when Black Death came racing at them.

A van, with reinforced steel crash bumpers, rocketing out of the side of the road. Smacking right into Lennon's car. Driver's side.

The Subaru flipped at least six times. Lennon lost count after the first two.

His first thought: Grab the gun.

His second thought: I don't have a gun.

They were all headed for the airport. He was headed for Puerto Rico. And Katie.

Glass shattered around his head, beads grinding into his scalp. The engine whined and complained and finally settled into a low hum.

Lennon had a limited view out of his side window. Grass— some burned, some green. Shoes. Walking toward the car.

There was a dull roaring sound. Lennon could smell his own burning clothes. The last thing he heard was himself, trying to scream.

FRIDAY P.M.

You should be able to strip a man naked and throw him out with nothing on him. By the end of the day, the man should be clothed and fed. By the end of the week, he should own a horse. And by the end of a year he should own a business and have money in the bank.

— RICK RESCORLA

Thousand Year Funeral

NDY STARED AT THE THREE BLACK CANVAS BAGS IN the back of the red Ford pickup truck. They looked like body bags. "That's the garbage?"

"Yeah," Fury said. "And it's all gotta go down that pipe over there."

Andy looked at the bags again, trying to discern human forms. The first two looked like bodies. He stopped himself. This was ridiculous. Just because his friend was named Fieuchevsky, and that he sometimes did favors for his mobster/gasoline-distributor father didn't mean . . .

"C'mon," Fury said, clapping him on the shoulder. "We gotta be onstage in a couple of hours. Let's get these bags down the pipe, have a beer, then get on 73."

Andy Whalen and Mikal "Fury" Fieuchevsky were the keyboard and bass players, respectively, for a cover band called Space Monkey Mafia. Fury had come up with the name after listening to Billy Joel's *Storm Front* drunk. All through March—Thursdays, Fridays, and Saturdays—the band was playing a resort hotel in Wildwood, New Jersey. It was mostly dead, but some people took advantage of off-season package deals, and those people liked to have live bands in the bar; the other nights were filled with karaoke.

Fury's father was friends with the owner and that had helped them land the gig. Occasionally, Fury had to go off and run errands for his father. Take this here, pick up this there, and tonight, dump this down here. Fury had called Andy at his dorm room at La Salle University a few hours ago, and since he had nothing better to do before the drive to Wildwood, he agreed to lend a hand.

"Which pipe?" Andy asked. There were three of them, sticking out of a long block of cement, under a blue tarp raised like a tent. They were on a construction site on the Delaware River, on the Camden, New Jersey waterfront side, right in the shadow of the Benjamin Franklin Bridge. Cool March air picked up some extra chill from the water and blew hard and fast across the riverfront. Andy wanted to go back and put on his windbreaker.

"The biggest one—the one on the left."

Andy saw it. It was roughly the diameter of a manhole cover. The other two pipes looked much smaller.

"C'mon. Grab one end of this."

Andy walked over to the back of the Ford and grasped the end of one of the bags. Fury reached in and grabbed the other end, then nodded. Together, they lifted, and damned if it wasn't heavy. The bag felt like it contained one big, thick piece of garbage, like a side of beef. Again, the words popped into Andy's mind: *dead body*.

The two of them took baby steps across the concrete until they reached the big pipe. Fury tipped his end down first, resting it on the lip of the pipe. "Ready?" he asked Andy. Andy nodded, and they heaved. The bag disappeared from view. Andy heard black vinyl rubbing against cold steel, then a muted *thud*, like a sandbag hitting a mound of soft dirt.

"One down, two to go," Fury said.

"This looks like a construction site. Aren't they going to find this stuff in the morning?"

Fury smiled and paused to rub imaginary pieces of lint from his black Z. Cavaricci pants. Cavariccis had been out of style for at least ten years, but Fury kept wearing them anyway. Andy thought Fury must have purchased them in bulk back in 1991.

"Next week," Fury said, "there's going to be another forty feet of concrete poured over this slab. That children's museum is going here—that 'Please Touch Me' joint? There's got to be a thick enough foundation to lift the museum up over river level. So whatever's buried here stays here for at least sixty years. My dad said that's how long the museum's new lease runs. The city made the developer agree to it—pretty much float the bill forever."

"Must be some garbage."

Fury picked up the sarcasm. "It's just garbage, Andy. Two more bags, and you can forget all about it."

They walked back to the Ford and again grabbed another black bag. Only this time, Andy's hands flew away, as if he had been burned.

"Hey, Fury?"

"What's wrong?"

"This garbage is, uh, breathing."

Fury stared at the bag, then looked up. "Go in the front of the truck, in the glove compartment, and bring me that small leather case in there. Okay?"

"Didn't you hear me? Look at this thing."

"I heard you, man. Just go get me that case, then grab a Rolling Rock and go for a little walk. Finish up and come back, and we'll get the fuck out of here and go play some music."

Andy's blood turned to ice water. He looked at the bag again—he couldn't help it, after all, it was *fucking breathing*—and then back at Fury.

"Jesus, man. Just level with me. Is that a fucking body in there? Did we just dump a human bod—"

"Shut up, Andy. Just shut up. They're deer. My dad went hunting, and I guess he didn't kill this one all the way. Now please, get me the bag and take a walk."

Andy turned away. The night sky, painted behind the tops of the Society Hill Towers across the river, looked blacker than usual. What should he do now? There was not much he could do now. Andy went to the front of the truck, opened the door, popped the glove compartment, and grabbed the small leather case. It was heavy, as if there was a dense stone tucked inside. A stone. Or garbage. Or a deer, still breathing.

He took the gun—yes, he could call it that now, what the fuck, he'd walked through that door already—and then snapped up the glove compartment lid.

Behind him, Fury yelped.

Andy clutched the case to his chest and ran around the truck. A bare human arm, somewhat streaked with blood, had reached out of an opening in the black bag and was in the process of trying to strangle Fury to death.

Some deer.

For a second, Andy wondered if he should open the case and take the gun. But then he realized he wouldn't know what to do with it—he was raised by two former hippies who didn't allow toy water pistols in the house, let alone real firearms. He carefully put the case on the ground and looked for the nearest available weapon that didn't require bullets.

There. A five-foot section of two-by-four.

Andy grabbed the two-by-four and ran over to Fury, who was wrestling with the bag on the ground. Hoisting the two-by-four above his head, Andy swung it down as hard as he could. The bag jolted, then jolted again as Fury managed to swing his knee up in the middle of the bag.

"Hit 'im again," said Fury, breathless.

Andy complied, and heard the distinct sound of something cracking. He didn't know if it was the wood or the thing inside the bag. Regardless, the bag started jolting again, almost spasmodically. Fury scrambled backward a bit, out of reach of the arm sticking out of the bag, then started launching punches into the top of the bag, spitting and cursing with each blow. Eventually, the bag stopped moving.

"Help me get this into the pipe," Fury said, rising to his feet.

Andy just nodded.

Together, they lifted the bag and shuffled over to the open pipe. The arm hung out of the bag, pointing to the ground like a dog's tail.

"Jesus Christ," Andy said.

"Don't say anything," Fury said. "We'll get this straightened out, go play our job, and drink beers after that until we can laugh about this."

"I don't think I'm going to laugh about this."

"Yeah, well."

Andy looked down at the bag and wondered about the guy inside. Andy was no fool. He knew that Fury's dad was a *vor* in the Philadelphia branch of the Russian *mafiya,* with a legit front as a club owner and a gasoline distributor in the Northeast Philly area. So this dead dude in the bag must have pissed off the Russian mobsters for something. He couldn't tell much from the arm hanging out. A white dude, thin but muscled. No needle marks. Maybe he welshed on a bet or something, or got greedy. Or maybe he was a lawyer they didn't need anymore. Andy looked for a watch or rings, but didn't see any. The Russian had probably stripped him of jewelry, anyway, either to hide identifying marks or pawn it. Then again, there were three bags. Unless the Russians saved up their bodies for mass disposal, these three guys were into something together. Andy hoped to God they weren't cops. His uncle was a cop, up in the Fifteenth District. Andy had made an uneasy moral peace with playing in a band with the son of a Russian mobster, but there was no way he could stomach the thought of—

The fingers on the arm twitched.

"Shit."

A fist was formed.

"What?"

The body in the bag jackhammered his fist into Fury's nuts.

That end of the bag dropped, which yanked the black plastic right out of Andy's hands. He took a few confused steps back, watching the hand reach around and grab the zipper. Andy could imagine the zipper being lowered, and seeing his cop uncle inside, bruised and bloodied. The blood in his veins chilled.

But when the zipper came down, it revealed a naked white guy Andy didn't recognize. The guy was bruised and bloodied all to hell, but he looked both pissed and calm at the same time. He stood up out of the bag, and Andy saw that he was *really* naked. Not even wearing skivvies.

Fury was writhing on the cement floor. This guy had really nailed him.

"Stop," Andy said, holding his hands out in front of him.

The naked guy staggered a bit. The punches and kicks and hits by the two-by-four seemed to have had an effect on him, after all. He fell to his hands and knees and visibly shivered. Then he looked up at Andy, hand outstretched in a *hold on a minute* position.

"Pound him, Andy!" yelled Fury, his voice strained and slightly higher than usual.

The naked guy was shaking his head *no*. He gestured with his right hand as if he were holding a pen and writing a note. What was he trying to say? Did he want to sign something?

"For fuck's sake, hit him!"

There really wasn't much of a choice. If Andy didn't do something, Fury would anyway. And God knows how pissed Fury's *vor* father would be if Fury told him Andy had hesitated to help. For better or worse, Andy was Fury's guy. Andy took a few steps back, found the two-by-four, and approached the naked man.

There was no pleading in his eyes. Just waiting. Almost a dare. Maybe even a glimmer of disappointment in there, too.

Andy swung the two-by-four like a T-ball bat, imagining the naked man's body as the T and his head as the ball. *Hard.*

The
Cold
Steel
Grave

LENNON WOKE UP AGAIN WHEN THE LIP OF THE PIPE scraped his chest. The hazy memories of the last few minutes loaded themselves back into his brain. It was all pain and fuzz and white noise, and flickering images of the inside of a black vinyl bag, and beatings, and looking at some dumb college kid, and then blackness again. He reached out to grab something, anything. His fingers scraped against concrete, then slipped around cold steel.

Shit.

The pipe.

The memory came back. These two jokers were dumping bodies down a pipe. Holden's body. Bling's body. Now, his body. *Whatever's buried here stays here for at least sixty years.*

His fingers found the edge of the pipe, and he clamped down as forcefully as he could.

"Let go fucker," a voice hissed, and he felt a fist hammer the base of his spine. Lennon's arms and hands went numb, but he kept holding on. The fist pounded his back again, and then his ass. Then more fists. Someone grabbed his legs and hoisted them up in the air. Then a fist smashed into his balls, and the fight was over. Lennon's fingers released their hold on the pipe and he felt himself sliding down it.

Arms, legs, *out*. That was the only thing he could do. Skin slid against steel. Lennon pushed his arms and legs out farther, as hard as he could. Flakes of acned rust on the inside of the pipe caught against his skin, shredding it. But it also slowed his descent. A few panicked seconds later he stopped falling.

Lennon was naked, upside-down in a construction pipe by the Delaware River, arms and legs torn to shreds and his testicles hiding out somewhere in the vicinity of his rib cage . . . but he had stopped falling. He'd take victory where he could get it.

Adrenaline flooded his bloodstream. He would have loved to scream. Lennon pushed harder against the confines of the inner pipe. He wasn't going to fall. No fucking way.

"He's stuck," a voice said up above.

Pause.

"Shit."

Another pause.

"You're *dead,* motherfucker, so you'd better give up now and drop. You want a bullet? That it? A nice couple rounds of hot lead up your ass, finish things off nice and quick?"

Lennon pushed harder against the pipe wall. This was no way to die.

"Get that two-by-four and see if you can push him down. I'll get the gun."

The slab of wood made a bonging sound against the side of the pipe. Then Lennon felt a hard jab on the back of his left thigh. Then another, more forceful this time. The rust dug deeper into his skin. The wood slammed into his butt cheek, painfully, almost causing Lennon to let go.

The next jab missed his body, rushing into the void between Lennon's chest and the pipe wall.

This was it.

Praying that three limbs could hold him up, Lennon's left hand whipped out and grabbed the wood. He felt it jerk upward, but Lennon held firm, then yanked back downward. The force of his pull almost dislodged him from the pipe entirely, but he held on as the rust plunged even deeper into his skin.

The two-by-four was in his hand now; the guy above had lost it.

"Shit. He just grabbed the two-by-four."

"It don't matter," said the other voice. "Fucker's going *down*."

Lennon looked up past his body to the opening of the pipe. A revolver was pointed back down at him and a meaty thumb started to pull back the hammer. So he did the only thing he could.

He shoved the two-by-four upward as hard as he could.

Wood snapped the guy's wrist. Surprised him completely. Hand popped open. Revolver tumbled out and down. Barrel caught the lip of the pipe. Weight of the gun dumped it inward. The gun fell down the pipe.

The gun landed on the underside of Lennon's genitals. He let go of the two-by-four, then reached around for the revolver. Grasped it. Grasped it like a fifteen-year-old with his first tit.

Come on, fucker. Take a look.

Look down.

His shaking thumb pulled back the hammer.

"Aw, you son of a bitch—"

The guy looked.

Lennon squeezed once, and the guy's head sprayed apart.

He could hear the other guy screaming, but that wasn't his concern now. Lennon had heard the two of them talking before. The guy he'd just shot was obviously the semipro; the other guy seemed to be along for the ride and needed directions at every turn. And now he'd lost his boss, his two-by-four, and the gun. Hopefully, they didn't have another gun. Lennon wouldn't have to worry about him for the time being.

Now his worry was getting out of the pipe.

There seemed to be two ways out. Some smart, clever way, and some exhausting, painful, bloody way.

Lennon couldn't think of any smart, clever ways, though he tried. He thought about slowly gliding farther down the pipe, expending precious skin real estate, but eventually hitting the bottom, where maybe he could dig until he hit water, then hold his breath and float back up to the surface like a cork. But there was no way of knowing what was below. Might be tightly packed mud; might be bedrock. This wasn't his river—fuck, this wasn't his city. Lennon then thought about slipping down farther until he found the two-by-four again, breaking it apart and trying to wedge pieces up in the pipe, and then using them as a makeshift ladder. But again, there were no guarantees that his strength would hold, or that the two-by-four could be broken. Most likely, it was fresh, strong wood; this was a construction site.

Upside-down, the blood continued to rush to his head. He couldn't hang like this forever. Enough blood in the brain and some foolish idea would seem reasonable, and then he would die. And this was a stupid way to die.

So it was down to the exhausting, painful, bloody way: Push hard, shimmy upward, and hope his skin held out until the surface.

It was the only sane option.

And hey, nobody ever said crawling out of your own grave would be easy.

Fifteen minutes later, Lennon's toes scraped the lid of the pipe. He pushed hard one last time, pressed his legs out in the air, and wrapped them around the pipe's edge. His muscles had been worked beyond exhaustion, ripped and burned and crying out for rest to repair themselves, but he pushed them one last time, clenching his entire body up to gain the leverage to grab the lip of the pipe with his hands and finally, to pull himself out. Lennon flipped over, stumbled on his heels, then collapsed to the concrete.

The other guy was there waiting for him.

He looked like he'd been crying, but the tears were ten minutes in the past. Since then he'd been doing some thinking. Some hard thinking. The kid—Lennon saw that now; the guy was just a college kid, or something—must have thought about the many ways to resolve the evening. Dump his buddy down on top of Lennon, then clear the fuck out? Dump cinder blocks and any shit he could find down the pipe and hope that did the trick? Or just call the cops and try to explain things?

But it looked like he'd decided on something different. The kid held out a notebook and a pen.

"I know you can't talk," the kid said. "You were trying to tell me that before, weren't you? So write down what we should do."

Lennon sat up, took the pen and paper, and thought about his options. The first thing that came to mind was taking the pen, uncapping it, then jabbing the business end into the kid's neck. But that would mean grabbing his head and hoping the arterial spray went in a different direction, and besides, Lennon wasn't sure he had the muscle power left to do any of that. Maybe not even to uncap the pen.

Then again, he needed rest and answers. Maybe this kid could help him with the first thing.

Lennon wrote: *Who are you?*

The kid read the note, and a grim smile floated across his face. "My name's Andy Whalen. I'm a senior at La Salle. Here, I'll show you." Andy pulled a brown leather wallet that was beat to hell from the back pocket of his black dress pants and slipped out an ID card.

Lennon looked at the student ID card. True enough. Andrew Whalen, a senior at La Salle University. There was a magnetic strip on the back of the card.

"Look, I don't know who you are, and honestly, I don't care. I know that Fury's dad is involved in some gangster stuff, and you probably know more than I do, but—"

Lennon held up a finger to his lips. Then he started writing again: *Where do you live?*

Andy read. "Oh. I live on campus."

Dorm or apartment?

"A dorm. I'm a senior, but I like living down on South Campus. And there are no apartments down there, so I'm in St. Neumann."

Alone?

"Yeah, I got tired of freaky-ass roommates. I'm in a single."

That was all Lennon needed to know.

He jammed the pen into Andy's neck, aiming more toward the back so the blood wouldn't spray all over him. Andy looked genuinely surprised, up until the point his eyes fluttered shut and he passed out.

Years ago, Lennon would have felt bad about something like this. During high school, he'd devoured the biographies of guys like Willie Sutton and Alvin Karpis, gentlemen bank robbers who never fired a shot unless absolutely necessary—and civilians were absolutely hands-off. And that was still the way Lennon liked to run his bank jobs. The threat, but not the kill.

However, there was a truth that had eluded Lennon in high school. Something that guys he knew called "human law." It wasn't God's law, moral law, or even the government's law. It was a law as old as mankind itself, and law number one was this: If someone fucks with you, it is imperative you fuck them back. Andy Whalen seemed like a nice college kid. But he had also taken a two-by-four and tried to stuff him, naked, down an industrial pipe.

Andy Whalen had fucked with Lennon.

That's what he thought about as he stripped Andy of his clothes, then dumped his body down the pipe, followed by the body of his semipro buddy. First, he fished the wallet out of the black Cavariccis. *Mikal Ivankov Fieuchevsky* was the name, with a Philadelphia address.

about
the
Benjamin

THE CLOTHES WERE SNUG ON LENNON. ANDY HAD APproximately the same height and build, but not quite the same muscle development. But it was better than being naked. Or wearing those ridiculous Cavariccis.

If Lennon had been thinking clearly, he would have stripped Fieuchevsky of his clothes first. Because even though Lennon had the guy's wallet, he didn't have his truck keys. They were most likely in the front pocket of the dead guy's dress pants. And Lennon wasn't one of those criminal types who knew how to hotwire any car—just a few select makes and models. This wasn't one of them. Besides, he usually stuck to bank stuff, and the cars he used in getaways always had keys. So now he had to walk back into Philadelphia.

The only visible option was the big blue bridge: the Benjamin Franklin, built in 1926 to connect Camden with Philadelphia. Why they wanted to do that in the first place remained a mystery to Lennon. Camden was a bigger shithole than Philadelphia.

Lennon pressed two fingers to his neck. Not good.

He spat in the right-hand lane, lit Andy's last cigarette, and walked across the bridge. Halfway across, he noticed how much the bridge swayed and bucked. He never knew bridges did that. He'd never had to walk across them before. The jittering under his feet pissed him off.

Now that he'd had some cold air in his lungs and time to think, the real pain set in. Clearly, today's job had been sold to somebody. Guessing from the appearance of Mr. Fieuchevsky, it was Russian mob. Somebody had told them what they'd be hitting, how much, and plotted the exact getaway route. Which enabled them to stash a ram van along Kelly Drive, then rob the robbers, dispose of the bodies, and move on with life. Somebody had told them all of this.

The problem was that somebody.

Bling knew the heist details, and knew a bit of the getaway strategy. But nothing exact. No schedules, no maps, nothing.

Holden didn't know shit. Lennon had insisted on that.

So even if Bling and/or Holden had gotten hopped up on H one night and decided to spill their guts to a hooker, they wouldn't have been able to tell anybody shit about the Kelly Drive portion of the getaway plan. That, Lennon had kept to himself. He had told nobody else about it, not about his timing, his mapping, and his practicing.

Except for one person.

Katie.

And Lennon didn't want to think about that.

He didn't want to think about how weird she'd been acting lately.

Secretive.

Quiet.

No.

Rest first. Then thinking and planning. It pained him not to be able to call Katie right away, give her the code, let her know what had happened. Ordinarily, Lennon would be sick that she'd be worried sick. But he couldn't do that now. He had to rest and heal. Then think.

The Benjamin Franklin Bridge spat Lennon out just above Old City Philadelphia, a former slum that had been rehabbed in time for the 1976 bicentennial celebrations and was now enjoying a turn-of-the-century renaissance of hip restaurants, bars, coffee shops, and art galleries. Lennon didn't care about any of that right now. He was consulting the Philly map he'd stored in his brain.

There was supposed to be a subway terminus at Second and Market, which he could take to City Hall and transfer to another subway line, which in turn would spit him out in the north part of the city, near La Salle University.

Once he found Second Street, the rest was easy. Lennon hopped the turnstile just as a steel train rocketed into the station. The Market-Frankford El. He boarded it, avoided all stares, and rode it thirteen blocks to City Hall, where there was the free transfer—exactly as the maps had said—into an even grimier subway line. The printed map on the train wall told him that the correct stop for La Salle was Olney, just a few stops from the end of the line.

He emerged from the station and saw a white and blue painted bus with a thick "L" painted on the side. Campus bus. Lennon showed Andy's ID card to the driver, who gave him a funny look but didn't say anything. Like he gave a shit. The bus wound its way around rough-looking streets, which quickly turned into trees and dark fields. A passing sign read ST. NEUMANN. Lennon stood up and the bus driver let him off in front of a three-story gray slab of a building.

The front entrance was guarded by two turnstiles and a sleepy-eyed student hunched over a thick literature anthology. No campus guards anywhere. Lennon slid the ID card through the turnstile; it clicked. The student didn't look up. Past the lobby was a main hallway, and tacked to one of the bulletin boards was a directory.

A. Whalen was in Room 119. The hallways were deserted. After all, it was a Friday night in March. School was more than two months under way, and so were the parties. The room Lennon wanted had a push-button combination lock on it. Lennon lifted his foot—clad in one of Andy's Sketcher boots—and pounded the door to the right of the lock. The door opened. Lennon didn't bother to turn on the lights, or check the phone machine, or undress. He flopped onto the bed and closed his eyes.

The
Mayor
Dreams
of
Holmesburg

MCGLINCHEY'S WAS DRAPED IN HUGE PLUMES OF gray-tinged smoke, which was to be expected. It was 10 P.M. on a Friday.

"What's this?"

"Take a look." Mothers slid a sheet across the black Formica table.

Wanted by the FBI
Identification Order No. 744 565 D

Patrick Selway Lennon
With aliases: P.S. Lennon, Pat Lenin, Pete Thompson, Lawson Selway, Charles Banks, Ray Williams, "Len."

Description
Born August 22, 1972, in Listowel, Ireland. Five feet eight inches tall, 170 pounds, with dark brown hair and blue eyes. Occupations: cook, laborer, clerk, writer. Scars and marks: one and half-inch horizontal scar on back of left hand, three-inch scar on throat, brown birthmark on right hip. Due to a throat wound suffered during a previous bank robbery attempt, Lennon is unable to speak.

Caution
Lennon is probably armed and should be considered extremely dangerous.

It was an FBI Wanted poster, freshly printed from the Internet, and Saugherty noticed that the date on it was tomorrow. The lieutenant was giving him advance copy. Saugherty read it. "This is the guy from the bank heist this morning?"

"One of them, yeah." Mothers had a swallow of porter beer.

"I thought they were all black guys."

"No, just one of them—Harrison Crosby. His partner was one of those Eminem wannabes, name of Holden Richards. And the getaway driver was this mick—Lennon."

"Well, I hope the FBI catches them soon," Saugherty said. "Golly, do I miss police work. Frankly, I don't know how you can stand it. You want another beer? I'm thinking about one of those Memphis Dogs, too."

"Yeah, I'll have another. Stay away from those dogs, though. I've been coming here since those little colon bombs were only a quarter a piece, and I still regret every single one I ever ate. There's something else about this guy Lennon."

"What's that?"

"You know that girl who got smacked by the getaway car?"

"Yeah. She okay?"

"She'll recover."

"And the baby?"

"Not a scratch. But the girl is somebody important."

"To who?"

"To the mayor."

"Who is she?"

"A political operative. Lives in Holmesburg, over on Leon Street."

"I'm guessing he values her oral presentations."

"To the tune of $20,000. Just for bringing this asshole down. Word went out this evening at the roundhouse. I thought you might be interested, seeing how you were looking to put a deck on the back of your house."

"Nah, I'm past the deck thing. Now I'm thinking, feng shui. My whole house is out of spiritual alignment."

"Costs a lot of money to realign your spirit."

"Wait. It's not called spirit; some other word. *Chi*. That's it. My chi."

"Chi whiz," Mothers said. "So, Paul—can I tell the mayor you'll be investigating this case on a freelance basis?"

"You can tell the mayor that I'm a big fan of Holmesburg, and that I'm always looking out for its residents."

"The mayor will be pleased."

"Patrick Lennon will not," Saugherty said.

A swallow later: "The mayor doesn't want him alive, does he?"

Funicular

THE CONQUISTADOR'S INTERNET ACCESS WAS DOWN. Katie had to hire a driver to take her to a nearby Internet café to check the Philly news—no mean feat. It wasn't until late before the *Inquirer* posted the story. Bank robbery. Suspects still at large. $650,000 stolen. Promising leads, and the FBI promising a swift resolution. Which was complete bullshit. The FBI had no idea.

But then again, where was Patrick?

He hadn't told her the exact flight number into Puerto Rico; instead, he said, she should enjoy the resort and casino and the swimming pool and room service until he got there. Warm sun, instead of crisp Pocono mountain air. Katie had rented one of the exclusive guest cottages down the mountain from the main hotel and casino. To get to your room, you had to ride a cable car the resort called a *funicular*. She must have ridden the funicular a dozen times, up and down, up and down, admiring the clear blue ocean views and lush foliage that draped the mountains, and then in the dark, the boat lights that shimmered in the distance. She kept hoping she'd see Patrick walk across the casino floor and smile at her, and she'd know everything had gone okay. And then she'd take Patrick's hand and lead him back down the funicular—she'd probably joke about how many times she had ridden the fucking thing, and that it almost made her queasy, but that of course, *hah hah hah,* wasn't the only reason she was queasy. She'd lead him into their guest cottage, then uncork the bottle of Vueve Clicquot she'd prepared for the occasion, and then when he was relaxed enough . . .

. . . and then what?

Katie didn't know.

How do you put something like this?

She couldn't read the novel she'd packed—some Lorene Cary book about Philadelphia during the Civil War. It was the book that the whole city of Philadelphia was supposed to be reading at the same time. But she couldn't keep her mind on it. And she couldn't check the Internet without having to hire a cab, and she'd already done that in the past forty-five minutes.

So instead Katie stood on a chair and reached for the leather zip pouch she'd stashed up in the room's curtains, up out of sight, between the folds of the shears and the main curtain, tucked away in a Ziploc freezer bag and secured to the fabric with safety pins. Inside the leather pouch was her gun, a .38 German-made Beretta. She stripped it, cleaned it, reassembled it, re-hid it.

That didn't help, either.

There was a knock at the door. Katie made sure the gun pouch was out of sight and then looked through the keyhole.

Michael. A day early.

Jesus, if Patrick had shown up on time . . .

She opened the door, and couldn't help herself.

"I know, I know, I'm early, but—"

Katie didn't let him finish. She slid her hands under his arms and cupped his shoulders, then leaned forward, pressing her lips to his.

The
Bastard

LISA DIALED ANDREW'S CELL ONE LAST TIME, THEN GAVE up and called his dorm room number. Oh, God help that bastard if he is in his dorm room. She had driven two and a half hours all the way down to Wildwood to see Space Fucking Mafia at the Thunderbird Lounge, and guess what? No Andrew. No Fury, either—his thick-necked Russian partner-in-crime. That was half the band. The good half.

All that remained was the guitar player and the drummer, and neither of them sang. The pair joked about their bandmates finishing up on the Ozzfest tour, that they should be onstage any second. To fill the time, they played Ventures guitar-rock songs— "Walk, Don't Run," "Slaughter on Tenth Avenue"—pretty much the only thing you can do with just a guitar and drums and no vocals. By the end of the set, the lesser half of Space Fucking Mafia was desperate enough to play Christmas songs, Ventures guitar-surf style.

What the hell was Andrew thinking?

There she was, down there with her townhouse roommate Karyn—who she really didn't like all that much, but couldn't avoid inviting—and her best friend Cynthia, who had never seen the band but heard Lisa's endless bragging. Which made it all the worse. Lisa looked like a real asshole. Add the fact that Thunderbird Lounge was a bit of a dive, full of cheap white trash who took advantage of the spring rates and took their shore vacations early. Cynthia rolled her eyes every ten minutes; Lisa could time it.

Karyn, meanwhile, had found some loser with a goatee and a Weezer T-shirt and was huddled in a corner, tongue wrestling. The loser probably didn't know that just twenty minutes before,

Karyn, a world-class bulimic, had power-vaulted her fast food drive-thru dinner into the third stall of the ladies' room. Karyn was now drinking a vodka and cranberry, but even that didn't have a prayer of killing the taste of vomit. Maybe the loser was too drunk to notice. Or the film of Coors Light in his own mouth canceled out the taste. Lisa shuddered.

Lisa gave it another hour, then decided to drive home, speed-dialing Andrew's cell every fifteen minutes the entire ride home. Karyn had begged them to stay longer, but nothing doing. Halfway through the trip, Lisa wished she'd left Karyn behind. She kept dialing. Nothing. Just the voice message. The fucking bastard.

Dropped Cynthia home with a lame apology, then back to the townhouse with puke breath. Tried the cell one last time, then the land line. Got his answering machine. Nothing.

This wasn't the first time with Andrew. Just this summer, Fury had taken Andrew to an all-day drinking party with some Thunderbird waitresses they'd met—boy, don't even get her started on that one—and they'd somehow driven back to Fury's dad's condo up in Egg Harbor Township, a full hour away, to crash for a couple of hours. The problem was, they were due back down in Wildwood to play a Thunderbird gig that night. Oh, Andrew and Fury showed up, but two hours late, sleepy-eyed and still reeking of Jack Daniel's. That was the night Lisa had brought her mom down to hear the band. She swore then it was the last time.

So no, she wasn't thinking about Andrew being in a car accident, or some other tragic situation. Because she knew better. Fury had driven him off on some side adventure, and she was done waiting. Let Andrew fuck the Russian asshole, he prefers his company to mine.

"Andrew, if you're there, you'd better pick up the fucking phone, and while you're doing that, you'd better be thinking up one hell of a fucking excuse."

There was a long beep.

The Clean-Up Crew

OWN BY THE RIVER, THEY FOUND MIKAL'S TRUCK, TWO open body bags with no bodies inside of them, and a spray of blood. They were forced to report back to Mikal's father, by cell phone. It was supposed to be just a routine checkup, to see what the kid was up to tonight. He hadn't shown up for his gig down in Wildwood—a buddy had called it in.

"He's nowhere in sight?" Mikal's father asked.

No, they said.

"Is there blood inside his truck?"

No. Just around the construction site. Some tarp and concrete and pipes sticking out of the ground.

"There anything inside these pipes?"

Not that they could tell. Not without flashlights or anything. Probably not. But they could check. They hung up, promising to call back soon.

"Fuck."

"What do we do now?"

"Chill. Just chill the fuck out, that's what we do."

"I don't want to do that. Gotta think, gotta think."

Fifteen minutes later, they called Mikal's father back.

Mikal's appointment book was still in the truck, they said, and on today's page they saw a note for a meeting. The names: Patrick Lennon, Harrison Crosby, and Holden. The exact details of the meeting were not known, but these three names happened to be the names of three bank robbers who were suspected of stealing $650,000 from a Wachovia branch in Center City that morning. It was in the paper today. Didn't he see it?

This was bullshit. No such news story had made the papers. But Mikal's father didn't know that.

Mikal's father didn't know about *any* of this. This had been Mikal's deal.

"Bank rob-bers?" said the father, through clenched teeth.

They didn't have to see the man's face to know his teeth were clenched.

The first matter of business was to find Mikal. (Yeah, right.) They were instructed to split up: one guy to Mikal's townhouse in Voorhees, New Jersey and the other to his friend, this piano player named Andrew, to his house. He lived in the northeast, not far from where some of the crew made their homes.

"Let's go, then."

"You know we're not going to find shit."

"That's not our problem. The man speaks, we go. Let's go."

an Unfinished Boy

IKAL'S FATHER RETRIEVED AN ICE-COLD BOTTLE OF Stoli from his miniature office fridge. He poured a drink to his son, who'd been so eager both to please his father and pursue his art at the same time. Sitting in some recording studio in downtown Philadelphia, along the waterfront, were the tapes of Mikal's unfinished rock album. Mikal's father had paid $18,500 for two weekends of studio time, complete with professional engineers and mixers. It had been a late birthday present for Mikal. He had been so thrilled, and was due back in the studio the following weekend—it had to be postponed because of a performance at the shore. Mikal had just turned twenty-two.

Now, Mikal's father considered that $18,500, and considered how he'd pay ten—no—one hundred times that amount just for the bitter pleasure of renting out a large soundproof room with concrete floors, two meat hooks, and a large industrial hose for cleanup afterward. He wanted those three bank robbers run through electric meat grinders and the remains doused in gasoline and burned.

Mikal thought about sending someone into the studio to take the tapes, just so that the robbers could listen to the music. In the spare moments when they weren't screaming for their lives.

Forty-five minutes later, his cell phone rang. It was his employees. They had discovered that someone was sleeping in Mikal's friend's dormitory room. And it wasn't Mikal's friend.

above

and

Below

LENNON HEARD THE WRENCHING OF STEEL AND HIS eyes snapped open. Once again, recent memories took their time returning. His aching hands felt the single bed beneath his body, and he knew he wasn't in his own bed. He was in a small room. The pale light filtering through a window to his right revealed that much; there was a wooden dresser and a desk. A dormitory room. The name Andrew Whalen popped into Lennon's head, then everything came rushing back.

The steel cried out again, and something heavy thudded to the ground outside of his window.

Lennon sat up, his deadened muscles protesting the motion, screaming for him to lie back down for another few minutes or months or years, but he had to see. He looked through the glass, which was protected by steel safety bars, and down one floor. There were three men dressed in black coats with knit black caps over their heads. One of them held a crowbar the size of an Arthurian broadsword.

They had pried the bars off the window and were preparing to enter the room below.

Andrew Whalen's room. The Russians.

Lennon had taken a chance and picked the room directly above Whalen's. In a building like this, singles were likely to be placed on top of other singles, doubles on doubles, and so forth, so heat ducts and plumbing lined up. Whalen's room was too risky—somebody was going to miss him soon enough and show up looking for him. Another single room was a smarter bet. People who lived in singles were either loners who went home on weekends, or seniors who had friends or girlfriends on campus elsewhere. It wasn't Lennon's safest move, but it was better than wandering the streets of a strange city, looking for shelter. His crew's "safe" apartment in West Philly should be assumed compromised. There was no place else for him to go.

Lennon watched the men enter the room. Then he heard a scream. But just for a brief second. He thought about trying to take a closer look, to see what he was up against. But he was in no condition for that. Better to stay here, regroup, rebuild, and work the problem with a fresh mind and body in the morning.

Lennon rolled back over and went to sleep, trying hard not to think of Katie.

Police

Positive

SAUGHERTY STOOD AT THE CORNER OF SEVENTEENTH and Market at 4:00 A.M., drunk off his ass, his belly full of beer and whiskey, thinking about bank robbery. I'm a bank robber, he thought to himself. Whoo-hoo-heee. I'm going to jack up this jug here, a Wachovia. Breeeeee-hawww. Where do I go afterward? If I'm a clever guy, I try to find my way out of the city without getting caught in any jams. This being Center City Philadelphia, good freakin' luck with that.

But the newspaper story Mothers had given him in the bar had explained that. The team was crafty—they'd set up phony window-washer horses all up the west side of Seventeenth Street, which allowed them easy access to JFK, and then to . . . to where? That was the $650,000 question. JFK led directly to Thirtieth Street Station and on-ramps for I-76, but that was one of the most congested points in the city. Smart guys like the Wachovia crew wouldn't go there. But they were headed up JFK for a reason. Only a few streets lie between Seventeenth and Thirtieth—most of the streets in the Twenties were stopped because of train tracks and the river. Wee-hew, I'm a bank robber, where do I go?

Saugherty looked in his wallet. He still had over $200 cash in there. Mothers had tossed him a line of credit.

He hailed the next cab headed down Market Street. He was in no mood to sleep and no condition to drive.

The
Hookup

THE PHONE RANG. LENNON'S GUMMY EYES FLICKERED open. It took a second, but everything came back to him quickly this time. Most important, the reason for the phone ringing.

The alarm he'd set had been tripped. Someone wanted back into the room.

It hadn't taken much. Lennon had scribbled a few words on a piece of paper, then taped it to the door of room 219: "Dude—I'm hooking up. Call first. PLEASE."

Lennon had wanted some kind of warning, just in case the occupant of room 219 were to return sometime this evening. Every male college student had an unspoken set of rules in regards to getting lucky with a member of the opposite sex. (Lennon had never graduated from college, but he'd had enough of it to glean this nugget of wisdom.) If you were a true friend, you'd always allow your buddy the use of your room for the purposes of carnal acts. Hell, you'd even allow a complete stranger who lived in your hallway the use of your room for immoral acts. Only a total dick would raise a holla over a brother gettin' some.

The note was vague enough—*Dude*—to warrant at least a call. That was why the phone was ringing.

The occupant of 219 wanted to come back, and wanted to make sure it was safe.

Lennon bolted upright and his entire body screamed back at him. There was no time. He snatched up the plastic bag full of clothes he had prepared before he had lain down and exited the dorm room. He took the staircase down one flight, slowly walked down the main hallway, and went into the men's room. There were six shower stalls inside, three on each side. Lennon chose one at random and used it to dress.

The clothes he'd picked out of the student's closet were purposefully random. A black White Stripes T-shirt, a gray Penn State sweatshirt, and a pair of ill-fitting Vans. He kept Andrew Whalen's black dress pants—they fit better than anything else he saw in the closet. He had also taken a Timex Indiglo watch, which was a far cry from the Swiss Army platinum watch the Russians had stolen, but at least it told the time. Which was 2:30 A.M.

Lennon felt like shit. He needed to find new shelter quick or he wasn't going to make it. Sooner or later he'd lose consciousness, and campus security would find him, and they'd call the cops, and everything would be over.

So Lennon walked outside the St. Neumann dormitory and sat on the front steps. He wished he had a cigarette; almost wished he smoked. He watched the darkness, and the occasional student walking past him, heading into the dorm, or to the parking lot situated directly across the way. It took forty minutes, but eventually he found what he wanted: a drunk student, pausing in front of the open driver's door of his late model Chevy Cavalier, debating whether or not to throw up now and get it over with or take his chances and start driving home before he passed out.

Lennon walked over to the lot quickly and made a big show of putting his hands out to help the student. He'd noticed the huge brown glass bubbles attached to poles dotting this part of campus—security cameras. As Lennon put his hand on the guy's back, he also nailed him once in the kidneys, which temporarily paralyzed him, and then another time in the windpipe, which temporarily rendered him mute.

Lennon pushed the student to the passenger side, relieved him of his keys, then started the Cavalier and drove out of the parking lot and down the hill to Belfield Avenue. Once the car nosed out of campus, Lennon stopped. Wait. He couldn't do this here—not in this neighborhood. Lennon drove back up the hill and took the loop that put him right in front of the dorms. He then reached over, opened the passenger door, and pushed the kid out. Campus security would spot him sooner or later. Besides, friends don't let friends drive drunk.

Now, shelter again. Lennon didn't know the neighborhoods well enough to know safe ones vs. not-so-safe ones, so he tried to find the only strip he knew: Kelly Drive. There were plenty of bridges and tree-covered canopies along the drive. One of them had to be good enough for temporary shelter. It took a while to find—the streets were hopelessly confusing in this part of the city, with burned-out warehouses and ruined shopping strips— but eventually Lennon nosed the Cavalier onto I-76, and then took the Kelly Drive exit. He found what he wanted within three minutes, then crawled into the cramped backseat to try to heal.

Sure, it was returning to the scene of the crime/betrayal, but it was also the last place the Russians would think to look for him. In a few hours Lennon would get up, steal another car, drive to the long-term lot, reclaim the money, and get the hell out of this city. Then he would figure out Katie, and the Russians, and how the two fit together. *If* they fit together.

Not too far down the road, Lennon's blood—spilled almost eighteen hours ago—soaked into the grass and mud beside the Schuylkill River.

Montana Extradition

UNCONSCIOUSNESS. BLACKNESS.
Then:

Tapping on glass.

Goddamnit. He was tired of being disturbed. The way his luck was running, it was probably a cop. Maybe that drunk La Salle kid had already called in his car. He should have found somewhere else to sleep. Or at least slept outside in the cold underbrush, away from the car. But that wouldn't have helped him heal any faster. Getting brained again and again hadn't done much for his logical thought processes. He was working this one through a brain fog.

"Hey in there," a voice said.

Lennon sat up and, once again, wished he'd done something differently. He wished he'd found a way to hold onto the Russian kid's gun.

A guy in a cheap sport coat was outside the car, leveling a Glock 17 at him. Classic cop gun—seventeen rounds, but only thirty ounces fully loaded, easy-pull trigger. Classic cop two-hand stance, too.

"Unlock the door," he said, his voice slurring a bit.

A plainclothes, out awfully late. Probably headed home from an after-hours cop bar, happened to catch sight of the car. Which was amazing—Lennon had hidden it well. But you never know what'll catch a cop's eye. Bastard probably smelled it.

Lennon sat up and caught sight of something odd parked down the hill on Kelly Drive. It was a Yellow Cab, headlights on, passenger door open.

"C'mon, buddy," the cop said.

Lennon shrugged, then reached over and unlocked the back passenger door.

The cop kept the Glock trained on Lennon, but briefly turned around to wave the cabbie off. Then he opened the door and slid in next to Lennon, right there in the seat. The pistol stayed on him the whole time. This cop was drunk.

"How's it going tonight? Me, I'm doing good. Gotta say, I keep stumbling into clover this evening. Had myself a couple of Memphis Dogs over at McGlinchey's hours ago, and I haven't had a single explosive diarrhea session yet. Maybe my stomach's adapting."

Lennon just stared at him. What did this guy want? This wasn't a vagrant roust. This was something else.

"You ever had a Memphis Dog? Only a quarter. Paired with a pint of Yuengling Black and Tan, it's the closest a Philly working stiff will ever get to nirvana."

Lennon slowly raised his hands, holding an invisible pen with one, and using it to scribble an imaginary note on the other. Then he made a slicing motion across his throat.

"Oh yeah, that's right. You can't talk, can you, Pat?"

Oh no. This cop. He was working the Wachovia job.

Fuck.

"Why is that, anyway? Your I.O. didn't elaborate. A bank job'd be my guess. Catch a bullet under the chin? Or did somebody try to double-cross you, slice you up like lunch meat, leave you for dead? Bank robbery can be such a dangerous profession. Frankly, I don't know how you can derive any real satisfaction from it."

Lennon didn't move. He just stared. Sooner or later, this guy would get to the point. And then he'd decide how much of a risk it would be to try to take the gun away from him.

"I'll bet you're wondering quite a few things, aren't you, Pat? You're probably wondering how I know your name, and how I found you so quickly. Well rest easy, brother. Your questions pale in comparison to the list of questions I have in my own head. Such as: Why *did* I find you so easily? Aren't you clever heist guys supposed to know how to get out of town quickly and quietly? I thought I'd be reading about your extradition from Montana at some point. But the fact that you're still here makes me think the job didn't come off as ducky as everybody thinks. Which raises even more questions."

The guy—Lennon wasn't exactly sure he was a cop anymore; he definitely used to be, but something about him said *early retirement*—paused to adjust the crotch of his pants. The pistol remained on target.

"Where are your partners? There were three of you. You're the wheelman, and the black guy and the wigger were the heavies. Maybe they're back waiting at the hideout up there in jigabootown, and you're staked out here for some reason. That's it, isn't it? The money's still here. You're waiting until it's safe."

The guy paused, waiting Lennon out. After about a minute of silence, Lennon simply shrugged his shoulders.

"Strong silent type, aren't ya? Well let me get to the point."

At long last.

"I could shoot you in the face right now, in the next very second, and make $20,000. Which is very nice money."

Definitely not a cop anymore. Not that cops didn't do shit like that, but he wouldn't be yapping about it. Of course, the fact that he was yapping about it also meant that this guy was going to shoot Lennon in the face, no matter what. Next, he was going to ask about the money.

"Or, we could go recover that bank money, when it's safe, and arrange a deal. Nod once if you understand me."

Lennon nodded once.

"Goody. So here's how we're going to—"

Lennon swatted his right arm outward, his wrist catching the guy's wrist and deflecting the Glock away, pointing it at the back windshield.

But not before the guy managed to squeeze the trigger. He was *fast*. He must have been prepared for Lennon to try something like this.

The shot felt like a hammer slamming his left shoulder. The

area exploded into numbness as his blood tried to circulate itself anywhere but there. The blood failed, and started geysering out of his shoulder, soaking the Penn State sweatshirt. It looked black in the darkness.

"Now see that," the guy said, calmly pulling his gun hand away from Lennon's weakening right arm. "We're not going to get anywhere like this. And I'm not ready to let you make your decision so hastily. A man should be able to think about these kinds of things in peace and quiet. Where's the keys to this car?"

Lennon shut his eyes, trying both to block the pain and plan his next move. There would be no point in trying the same stunt twice. He had to think.

The guy tapped him in the face with the still-hot barrel of the pistol. "Hey. Come on now. Simple question. Keys."

Keys. Above the driver's seat visor. Keys meant the guy wanted to drive him somewhere. It was a chance to think, to plan something. He couldn't drive with a gun on Lennon the whole time.

Lennon gestured to the visor. The guy smiled. "Well thankee greatly." He stepped out of the car, walked around to the driver's side door, opened it, and snatched the keys up. Then he walked around the back again and used the keyless button to pop the trunk. "Damn, Pat, you should see the shit back here," he called from the outside. "Sorry to say, this ain't going to be very comfortable."

It wasn't.

SATURDAY a.m.

Do I look like a bank robber to you?

— WILLIE SUTTON

Sickness and Wealth

KATIE LEFT MICHAEL IN THE COTTAGE AT 1:55 A.M. AND asked him to stay there until she called. He said it was okay; he had some loose ends he had to tie up anyway. He told her to be safe, and call him if anything got out of hand. He'd be there in a heartbeat. Katie said she'd be fine. She really didn't want to involve him in this.

At 6:10, Katie's flight from San José landed at Philadelphia International Airport. By 6:40, she was in a rented car, a black Buick Regal, her one piece of luggage stowed in the trunk. By 7:05, she was at Rittenhouse Square. By 7:08, she was knocking on the door of room 910 in the Rittenhouse Towers, a combination luxury hotel/condominium complex. At 7:10, the door opened.

"Katie?"

"Morning, Henry."

"Aren't you supposed to be on vacation?"

Katie pushed past him. The door led to a $1,275,000 three-bedroom apartment: ceiling-to-floor windows, revealing views of both rivers, parquet floors. Nice, but by no means the best apartment in the building. Henry Wilcoxson didn't like to live too ostentatiously. He was a semiretired jugmarker, a man who plotted bank robberies for other teams in exchange for a percentage of the profits. Wilcoxson had worked with Lennon years ago, which was how Katie had met him. The man had taught them both a great deal; he was the closest thing either of them had to a mentor.

Wilcoxson had settled in Philadelphia, despite the fact that he had once escaped two different prisons here—Eastern State and Holmesburg—back in the 1950s under a different name. Now he owned a number of restaurants and coffee shops in the city and suburbs, and except for rare occasions, was out of the business. Wilcoxson liked to dabble, offer advice, but not much else.

"Coffee? I was just making a pot."

"No you weren't. There's still sleep in your eyes. Have you heard anything?"

"No," Wilcoxson said. "Nothing that wasn't in the news. All signs of a successful conclusion. But I take it that Patrick didn't make it to your predetermined meeting place."

Katie didn't seem to hear him. She put down her luggage, then paced, gray-faced, around the apartment, idly looking out the window at the two gleaming blue Liberty Place towers. "Can I use your bathroom?"

Wilcoxson smiled confusedly at first, then looked at Katie again and remembered. "Of course."

The
Bible's
Hell

LENNON SHOULD HAVE PASSED OUT BY NOW. A GUNSHOT wound and a pistol-whipping in the trunk of the car—"Gotta keep you humble," the ex-cop explained—should have sent vital instructions to his brain to shut down already. But no. Lennon stayed painfully conscious, albeit in a thick brain fog, the entire time: across the city's bumpy streets, into a garage, out of the trunk, and onto a thick wooden door which rested on two short metal cabinets.

He was strapped down by chains and thick elastic bungee-type bands, the kind you use to strap furniture to a roof. The ex-cop was careful to steer clear of Lennon's shoulder and lower right arm, but managed to strap him down every other way.

He had no idea where in the city he was—if he was even in the city. Or who this guy really was, and what was next.

Lennon did know one thing: this fucker was not getting the money. If he was going to die, it would be with $650,000 to his name.

"You know, I was just standing here all worried about trying to find a gag for you," said the ex-cop. "But that's not really a worry now, is it?"

The garage was a two-car model. The stolen Chevy Cavalier sat in one slot; Lennon was strapped to the table in the other. This guy—if he even lived here—used the garage as storage for tools and random junk. An ergonomic shovel. A wet/dry vac. A bike frame. A rusted gas grill with tank. Shelves lined every available wall, and they were packed to the point of being swaybacked.

"We've got a ticking clock here. If you don't see a doctor soon, you're going to bleed to death. Believe me, I know. I've seen guys take a dozen slugs and live. But just one GSW, left untreated, will kill you. Even if the bullet passed all the way through—which I think it did, because there's a nice hole in the backseat. Still, that shoulder of yours is going to be trouble in a couple of hours. And let me say, it doesn't look all that great now. It's starting to stink."

His captor placed a Bic ballpoint pen in Lennon's right hand and slid a legal pad beneath it.

"Just write down where I can find the money. I go check it out and make sure, then come back with a doctor."

Lennon just stared at him.

"Now I've got to come clean with you—there's no deal to be made. That was just some shit I said to get you to cooperate. Now you've got a stronger incentive: staying alive. You do want to stay alive, don't you?"

Honestly, at this point, Lennon wasn't exactly sure.

"Of course you do. And being alive in federal custody is a lot better than being buried in the middle of Pennypack Park." The guy wrapped his meaty hand around Lennon's writing hand and squeezed. "Do you know what 'Pennypack' means? 'Deep dead water.' I never knew that until recently, and I've lived up here my whole life."

A pause.

Lennon started scribbling on the legal pad.

"There we go," the guy said, leaning over to take a look.

He frowned.

"Oh. Fuck me, is that it? Okay, pal. Have it your way." He disappeared, and Lennon heard a door slam.

Immediately Lennon knew he'd made a mistake. He should have swallowed his rage and scribbled down a plausible location—hell, point him to any parking lot downtown and give him a phony make, model, and license number. That would at least take him out of the picture for a while; from his guesstimates, it was about a thirty-minute drive between where he was now and downtown Philly.

Lennon thought about that name—Pennypack Park. That rang a bell. Lennon consulted the map of Philly he'd stored in his brain for the job. Nothing downtown. Nothing in South or West Philly, either; he'd scoped those areas for possible getaway routes. Maybe it was near suburbs. Pennypack, Pennypack. The name bugged him. In for over six hundred thousand, out for a pennypack. But where did that fit into the map of Philly? The biggest park in the city was Fairmount, and Kelly Drive shot up right through the middle of that. The guy had driven too far to be near Center City still, unless he had doubled back to be clever.

Lennon heard the guy's weight creaking on the floorboards above. Probably his kitchen, right above the garage. Water and gas pipes snaked around and up into the ceiling. He could hear his voice above, murmuring. Talking on the phone to somebody.

A short while later, Lennon found out who.

Nightmare in Red

I HAVE NEWS," WILCOXSON SAID OVER THE CELL PHONE. "I'm not going to like this news, am I?" Katie asked. She was walking around Rittenhouse Square, sipping a paper cup of decaffeinated tea, trying hard not to lose her cool. It was getting harder and harder every day—emotions, body temperature, everything out of whack. She was tempted to call Michael, but that was weak. She just got here. She could figure this out by herself.

"No. The latest deal fell through."

She knew the code, but didn't understand what Henry was saying. The Wachovia bank had been robbed. It was in all of the local papers.

"According to the business section," she said, "the deal went through."

"Indeed. Initially. But it fell through during the financing, and someone else stepped in."

"Someone on the inside?"

"No, an outside company."

"Who?"

There was a pause. "I don't know if I should reveal that kind of information, since it hasn't been reported anywhere. In fact, not even the SEC has receiving filings yet."

SEC = FBI.

"Fucking tell me," Katie said.

"Look, let's have lunch and talk about this in greater detail. There are other options for you. And your family."

"Who the fuck was it, Henry?"

He sighed. "Your husband wouldn't like me discussing his business with you like this, but all things considered, maybe it's better you hear it from me. It was a foreign company, with increasing financial interests in this part of the state."

"Do you mean the company based in Milan?"

"No. Uh . . . St. Petersburg."

Katie was silent. Russians?

What were the Russians doing involved in this? Think, think. The hijacked funding was meant for urban renewal. Maybe the Russian mob had their hand on the building and trades folks, or were on tap to do the demolitions. Shit. Katie knew little about Philadelphia—just the physical layout and a few rudimentary historical facts, such as the fact that the Italian mob had been decimated in this town over the past twenty years. Katie had no idea the Russians were such a force. Think. What was their interest here? How did they find out about the heist?

And what did they do with Patrick?

"Do you have a PR contact for that company?"

"Oh Jesus," Wilcoxson said. "Katie, no."

Say Hello To Mothers

A HALF HOUR MUST HAVE PASSED. LENNON COULD feel the blood spurting out of his shoulder in slow, steady waves. He grew bored with making an inventory of the items in his captor's garage—channel locks, hammers, picture frames, band saw, power screwdriver . . . but at least it kept his mind off Katie. For a few moments. Until he started thinking about Katie again.

Lennon had to rethink this. There was some other leak—not Katie.

Why, then, did she pop into his head the first moment he realized there'd been a double cross?

Her behavior over the past month. Weird. Katie was not a secretive girl—not to him, anyway. It wasn't one huge thing, just a series of small, seemingly inconsequential things. Sudden errands to run. Phone calls that suddenly turned polite after he returned home. The "history" on their Internet browser routinely erased.

Stop it, Lennon. Think about who else could have sold you out. Not Bling. Bling was dead.

But you didn't open the body bag, did you? You don't even know both body bags went down the pipe. Where were Holden and Bling during the crash? The backseat. Where did the van hit? Pretty much Lennon's driver's side door. Did the crash knock Holden and Bling out? Or did Holden and Bling owe the Russian mob money, and decide to cash in their getaway driver to settle the debt?

No, not Bling. Bling was almost as ridiculous as Katie.

Unless it was Bling and Katie.

No.

Think about the bleeding first. How to stop the bleeding. How to get unstrapped from this table. How to get the hell out of this garage.

Then answers.

A door opened behind him. "I can't believe it," a voice said. "Pat, are you still awake?"

Lennon stared at the ceiling.

Someone slapped him in the face. "Hey, come on. Don't be rude. I've brought along a friend. Patrick Selway Lennon, bank robber and fugitive, meet the man who's going to get a few answers out of you."

The other guy walked around the table, eyeing Lennon up and down. He was a big guy. Not fat or especially strong-looking, just big and wide and tall. He had a thick black moustache tucked under his nose, a sleepy-eyed expression on his face, and a Borsalino hat on his head. The man looked tired, mean, and permanently rumpled.

"Say hi, Pat," the ex-cop said. "Oh, that's right, I forgot. Sorry."

The big guy turned away and started looking around the garage. "You got a drop cloth or something?"

"Hmmm. I don't know. Wait—I painted the back bedroom a few months ago, and the set came with a plastic drop cloth. Never use 'em, because they're for shit. Will that do?"

"Yeah. Unfold it and put it over here, to his right, on the floor and over anything you don't want splattered."

His captor found the plastic drop cloth and unwrapped it. His big pal unholstered a Sig Sauer pistol from under his right arm and yanked back, popping one into the chamber. His captor dropped out of Lennon's sight. There was the sound of crinkling plastic.

"Hey, Saugherty."

The captor's head popped up. "Huh?"

The big guy aimed and shot Saugherty in the chest. The man's fingers tensed on the table, scraping at the surface, and then his head flopped forward, as if on a hinge that suddenly decided to unfold the wrong way. Then a gurgle, fingers slipping from the table, then a thud on the floor.

Lennon looked up at the big guy.

The big guy stared back at him. "What, you waiting for an explanation?"

Lennon stared at him.

"Well, this is gonna be an extremely disappointing day for you."

The big guy disappeared and walked up the steps. The floorboards above creaked. He started making a phone call.

Disappointment City

NEVER SHOULD'VE TRUSTED THAT PRICK," MUMBLED A voice from the floor.

The ex-cop, Saugherty, was still among the living.

"Christ, does this hurt. Least he had the courtesy to have me put down some plastic. That way, my shit won't get messed up." He started to chuckle, then groaned. "Ah, don't make me laugh."

Lennon listened. Waited.

"You still with me up there? I know you can't talk or nothing, but how about a little cough? Maybe a grunt? A whistle? You don't need vocal cords to whistle. Or do you?"

After some consideration, Lennon coughed.

"At long last. Real conversation. I feel like Helen Keller's teacher."

Lennon coughed again.

"You know, you're one of the last great raconteurs, Pat. Brief, and to the point, but engaging nonetheless."

Lennon coughed—impatiently this time.

"Okay, okay. I don't know if I'm going to remain conscious much longer. I'm seeing gray splotches as it is. So, here's the deal. I'm going to hand you my piece, and you're going to try to shoot that double-crossing prick in the face."

Well, now. Looks like it was going to be a disappointing day for someone else.

"You understand me? Knock on the table with your free hand. I forget which one it is from down here."

Lennon tapped lightly with his right hand.

"Goody. Now I'm not going to try to bargain with you. I'm no fool. Just do me a favor. Man to man. You get out of this, you kill that prick, how about you let me live. Just leave me be, and I'll forget about you."

Whatever, Lennon thought.

"Honest. Cough if you understand. Hell, I don't care if you lie. I just need to know you understand me. And I'm going to count on the fact that you're a human being beneath all that."

Lennon waited a moment or two—he sensed that Saugherty wouldn't be satisfied unless Lennon appeared to be giving this some serious thought—then coughed.

"Enough said."

After some grunting and mutterings, Lennon felt a smooth polymer Glock slide against his fingers. The piece thumped on the table. He reached out with his fingers and turned it around, then wrapped his hand around the grip. There.

Welcome to Disappointment City. Population: the Gobshite Bastard Upstairs.

"You got it?"

Lennon coughed.

"Okay. Good. I'm going to kiss floor for a while. Wake me up when the fun starts."

Moments passed.

"Ah, Jesus," Saugherty muttered. "Ah, motherfucker."

It was a long wait. Whatever the big guy upstairs was doing, he was taking his time. Lennon badly wanted to ask Saugherty a few questions. Who was the guy? Another cop? He had the aura of cop about him. What were he and Saugherty planning to do? Probably torture the location of the $650,000 out of Lennon, split it, then get rid of him. This guy, Saugherty, didn't have the stomach for the torture thing himself, so he called in a heavy-hitter buddy of his. Someone he thought he could trust. Someone he'd misjudged.

Now the Big Guy. What was going through *his* head? Maybe the Big Guy wanted the $650,000 for himself. But that seemed to be too low a figure to risk killing a former partner. Either Big Guy was stupid and greedy, or there was something else going on. Lennon leaned toward the latter. He thought about what the Big Guy said. *This is going to be an extremely disappointing day for you.* That meant he had other plans for Lennon. If it was just about the money, Big Guy would have commenced torture proceedings immediately. He didn't. He went upstairs to call somebody. Who?

When the front door upstairs squealed and sets of heavy feet trampled into what Lennon imagined to be the kitchen, the answer came to him.

Shit.

Big Guy was in bed with the Russian mob.

Russian mob wanted the money.

Russian mob also probably wanted to talk to him about the dead boys in the pipe down by the river.

That's why he was still alive. To be tortured later.

Lennon remembered the pistol in his hand. He squeezed the grip.

"Christ on a cracker," Saugherty mumbled from the floor. "Sounds like a platoon up there."

Lennon tried to count footsteps, figure out how many he was dealing with, but lost track. He looked around the garage, hoping for an answer. A way out. Anything.

"I don't mean to be a downer, Pat, but I think you're a dead man."

Speed
Loader

PATRICK SELWAY LENNON MIGHT BE A DEAD MAN, thought Saugherty, but I'm not.

They keep underestimating you. They underestimated you right off the force, and they're still underestimating you now. Mothers, too, of all people. Shooting him in the chest. Mothers worked with him in the Fifteenth District back in the day. Mothers always teased him about not wearing his armor. Saugherty wanted it that way—the guy who said fuck you to Level II. Saugherty secretly wore it anyway.

He had noticed an interesting side effect to a steady diet of Jack Daniel's and pounds of bacon and beef burgers with no bun: rapid weight loss. Fucking Atkins. Amazing. Saugherty lost the fat, kept the muscle, and wore the armor without anyone knowing. Saugherty wore it all the time. It was his second skin. It was damn near a fetish, if Saugherty wanted to be honest about it. One more secret. One more way they kept underestimating him. Mothers popped him in the chest, just like a good cop is taught to do. Center of gravity. And yeah, the blow knocked the living shit out of him. But no permanent damage. Skin badly bruised, not broken. Saugherty had faked his writhing on the floor, but only to a degree. The shit *hurt*. Thankfully, Mothers didn't go for the insurance shot. Thought one bullet was all it would take. Now Saugherty was going to find out what was *really* going on.

Saugherty knew the mayor-porking-the-Leon-Street-chick thing was bullshit. The mayor was straighter than a grizzly's dick: a proud Baptist from North Philly, goo-goo eyes in love with his wife of thirty-five years. He had other shit he was involved in—namely, this cash disbursement in the neighborhood, which was a cover for some debt he owed old friends. White trim simply wasn't one of his vices.

At the time, Saugherty hadn't really cared. Mothers was offering decent money for a quick job, and that was that.

But now it was suddenly something else. Something worth more than $325,000.

Something that involved a large number of accomplices.

Saugherty was doubly glad he had given his gun to the mute bank robber. Originally, he had thought it was over-insurance: distract Mothers long enough to get off a clean shot of his own. That's right. Mothers hadn't even checked him for a weapon. His belt piece had gone to the mute guy, but Saugherty had kept a snub-nosed pistol in a short holster perched at the small of his back. Mute bank robber squeezes off a few rounds; Mothers takes one or two but returns fire, and Saugherty clips him from below. Perfect.

Now, Saugherty realized, giving up his gun to the mute was going to be essential. Let him make the first move, take the first hits. Saugherty tried to concentrate on how many footfalls he heard, how many guys were with Mothers.

If he were forced to guesstimate, he'd say three.

Hopefully, the mute could take out one, maybe two, before getting clipped himself. That left at least two for Saugherty. Not a problem, if he could surprise them. Mothers first—he was probably the most dangerous—then the others.

Saugherty reached down and wrapped his fingers around the hidden pistol.

"Hey," he called up to the mute. "Aim for the center of gravity."

The $650 Insult

THE TWO FATHERS SAT TOGETHER AT A BOOTH IN THE Dining Car on Frankford Avenue, near the Academy Road exit of I-95. It was early, early—nearly 8:00 A.M. It had been a long night. A flurry of phone calls that had roused them both from their beds. Another round of phone calls to get the facts straight. And finally, two more phone calls to arrange this breakfast.

"How is your Lisa?" Evsei Fieuchevsky asked.

"Fine, fine," said his guest, Raymond Perelli. "Your boys treated her fine."

"That's nice to hear."

"And . . . your boy?"

Fieuchevsky grimaced. "Still missing."

"Motherfuck."

"Yes. Mother. Fuck."

Lisa.

Mikal.

The fathers hadn't known about the connection between the two. Lisa Perelli had been dating La Salle University senior Andrew Whalen for three months—ever since the end of winter break, when one of Lisa's friends had dumped Whalen and she was there to pick up the pieces. They got along famously. Lisa already knew Andrew's ticks; she'd heard Kimberly complain enough about them. She knew how to circumvent them, use them, fashion him into what she wanted. Mostly.

By sheer coincidence, Andrew Whalen played in a rock band with Mikal Fieuchevsky, the son of a suspected Russian *mafiya vor* based in Northeast Philadelphia.

The Southeastern Pennsylvania Crime Commission did not see this as sheer coincidence. They had been wiretapping Andrew Whalen's dorm and home phone lines since January 10, 2003, when news of the Whalen-Perelli affair first made it back to headquarters. The Crime Commission saw it as a direct link between the dying Italian mob and the leaner, younger, tougher Russian mob. The relationship was a ruse, they reasoned; Whalen got his dick sucked at least three times a week (according to surveillance tapes and photos), and in exchange, acted as an intermediary between Evsei Fieuchevsky, suspected *mafiya vor,* and Ray Perelli, a capo with what remained of the pathetic Philly mob, passing messages and instructions and sometimes cash. Ray "Chardonnay" Perelli treated his young messenger well, the Crime Commission discovered. Aside from the cock-worship courtesy of his daughter, Whalen was treated to a vintage Yahama DX7-II to use during gigs. A birthday present.

The Crime Commission was dead wrong. Andrew Whalen was aware of Mikal's father's somewhat dubious background, but had no idea about Lisa. All he knew was that she was a bit possessive, yeah, but she was also the most sensual woman he'd ever been with. High maintenance, but with excellent performance. It was worth it. It kept him coming back to her. The DX7-II hadn't hurt, either.

"Here," Fieuchevsky said, sliding an envelope across the maroon Formica table. "This is to make up for damage we might have caused."

Perelli smiled. "You don't have to do that."

"I insist."

Perelli made a show of refusing the envelope, but took it after a few moments and slid it into his jacket pocket.

"There anything I can do for you?"

Now it was Fieuchevsky's turn to lay on the fake warm smile. "No, no. Our business is done. Enjoy your chipped beef."

"Hey, I wanna help."

This dance continued throughout Perelli's chipped beef—or, as he liked to call it, "shit on a shingle"—and Fieuchevsky's tomato omelet and three orders of bacon and Stoli on the rocks. It was awkward and ingratiating and cautious. It finally wound down to a graceful conclusion when Fieuchevsky slid an FBI Wanted poster, folded in threes, across the table.

"If you, or any of your people, have occasion to see this man," he explained, "I would be most appreciative to have a word with him first."

Perelli took the poster and slid it into his pocket. "I'd be delighted."

Fieuchevsky thought, Slovenly dago bastard couldn't find his cock under rolls of his meatball fat.

Perelli thought, Russian pricks are losing it. Time to get back into the game.

A cell phone chirped. It was Fieuchevsky's. He listened, then told Perelli that he had to be going. Perelli suddenly had to be going, too, and thanked Fieuchevsky profusely for the $8.95 breakfast.

Outside, in his silver BMW, Perelli ripped open the envelope.

His jaw dropped. It contained a personal check for $650. In the memo line were the words: "College window bars."

The fucking bars on the dorm window.

Three thick-necked Russkie goons come pouncing in on his daughter, and all the commie bastard has to offer is $650?

Perelli wanted to puke up his chipped beef. All over that Fieu-fuck-sky's car windshield.

And then he had the nerve to ask for a favor.

Find this guy. Patrick Selway Lennon. A bank robber.

Ah, fuck you, you Russian prick. Find your own asshole, then finger it a few times for good luck. Those Russian bastards, sweeping into town, acting as if they've run things since forever. Smirking over the flurry of indictments in the crazy summer of 2001. Then there were the goofy antics, like the cops finding that one-legged bag man under the bed of the boss's wife while the boss was on trial for his life. The Russians, picking over the spoils of a once-great empire.

Perelli drove away mad. *Really* fucking mad.

The

Third

Crew

WHEN THE BLACK GUYS WITH THE GUNS ENTERED the garage, Saugherty saw right away he had guessed right. There was Mothers, plus three other guys. Not that it made him feel any better.

Maybe the mute would get lucky and clip two of these guys. Leaving only two for Saugherty. Not great odds, but it could be done.

"Cut him out," said a voice.

Two dudes with blades started snipping the bungee cords off the mute. The mute had obviously hidden the gun somewhere for the time being. Come on now, Saugherty thought. Start spraying. Pop pop. One guy, two guys down. Leaving two for Saugherty. His gun hand was already getting sweaty. It was hard playing dead while steeling yourself up for action at the same time. His chest hurt, bad. He hoped he wouldn't have a muscle spasm at an inopportune moment.

Then, something unexpected happened.

The mute bolted from the table—an old thick wooden door Saugherty had found trash-picking in Mt. Airy years ago—and pulled it over on himself at the same time. He scuttled across the floor of the garage, the door on his back, looking like a crab trying desperately to hang onto its shell. The mute was trying to use the door as a shield.

The three guys with the guns laughed. They catcalled, "Hey, white boy. Where you going?" Who could blame them? It looked pathetic.

"That door ain't going to help you, Mr. Lennon," Mothers said, a smile on his lips.

The guys removed submachine guns from their puffy coats. Loaded clips. Switched off trigger guards. The two others had black semiautomatic pistols, which they yanked on to pump bullets into the chambers. The garage was full of the sound of clean sharp metal clicks. Just one submachine gun would be enough to cut Saugherty and the mute in half. Hell, these guys had enough heavy firepower to launch an assault on a police precinct.

"All we need is one arm," Mothers continued. "The rest don't matter. These guys here can surgically remove your limbs through that fucking door in seconds. You won't live long, but you'll live long enough to be useful to them."

The door wobbled. Was the mute finally going for his gun?

And if he was, what the fuck was he hoping to accomplish with it?

The situation had gone from *fucked* to *cluster-fucked*. The only tactical advantage Saugherty had was that all four men now had their backs to him. He could try to stand up and get off six rapid, clean shots into each . . . no, that was ridiculous. He couldn't possibly take down more than two without the others spinning around and spraying him into pieces.

The door lifted a few inches from the floor of the garage. The business end of Saugherty's Glock poked out.

The guys laughed even harder and readied themselves to take aim.

What the fuck was the mute thinking?

"Okay. Will somebody kindly remove this bastard's leg?"

Saugherty traced the barrel's aim. Across the floor of the garage, above Saugherty's head, behind him, and into what? He stole a glance.

The tank of his gas grill.

Oh no.

"Remove *this,* ya fuckin' arseholes," the mute said. He fired the Glock.

Out the Door

THE EXPLOSION POUNDED HIM BACK INTO THE WALL OF the garage, but the door held. Lennon could feel the heat trying to blast through the wood. It wasn't going to hold up much longer. It was probably already on fire. He slowly climbed to his feet with Saugherty's gun in his hand. He looked over the wooden door.

Saugherty's garage was an inferno. Pretty much everything inside was either blackened or ablaze, including the black guys with the guns. (Guess they weren't Russian mob after all.) One of them squirmed on the floor, and Lennon pumped a bullet into him. He scanned for other stragglers through the smoke. This was no time to be uncertain. He was neck-deep in murder. He might as well make the most of it.

But the fire was out of control. He had to get out now. He wasn't sure if *he* was going to make it much longer without losing consciousness. His body screamed, and his shoulder screamed louder.

The easiest way out: use the door.

The aluminum garage doors were already buckling. Lennon could hear it. So he hoisted the wooden door—it was a heavy son of a bitch—and used it as a battering ram. The door went through the aluminum, and Lennon followed behind. He released his grip on the door before it brought him down with it, and tumbled off to the side.

Fresh pain spiked through every nerve. Get up, get up, he told himself. His hair felt like it had been crisping over a barbecue pit.

He climbed to his feet and quickly assessed his surroundings. It was madly disorienting. Jesus, this looked like a suburban cul-de-sac. A yellow plastic Big Wheel was perched on a lawn across the way. It was a bright, sunny spring day. The sun burned his skin.

And behind him were five barbecued men—three of them probably gangbangers and the other two probably cops, or ex-cops. Lennon had a bullet in the arm, bruises and contusions all over his body. He also had a gun in his hand and $650,000 waiting for him in the trunk of a car in downtown Philadelphia.

Lennon started walking. He had to get away from the burning house, and away from eyewitnesses. Probably way too late for that. He already saw faces peeking from behind curtains, fathers stepping outside their screen doors.

Enough was enough. Nearly twenty-four hours had elapsed since the Wachovia heist. Now it was time to bring the getaway to a close.

The warm air sharpened his senses, or at least gave that illusion.

Orders of business:

Find a car.

Find a convenience store. Snag a long-distance calling card and a map of Philadelphia.

Dump some rubbing alcohol over his shoulder wound.

Wrap a tourniquet around it.

Pray to Christ nothing got infected.

Figure out where the fuck he was.

Call Katie's cell. Enough dancing around it. Thirty seconds on the phone would tell him what he needed to know.

Meet up with her. Or cut free, and worry about her later.

Arrange a way out of town, with the cash.

Never, *ever* visit Philadelphia again.

a Fond Memory of Hardship

SAUGHERTY PURCHASED HIS TWIN ON COLONY DRIVE IN 1988, with his then-wife Clarissa and five-year-old boy. The price then was $65,000, which made for slightly uncomfortable mortgage payments on a cop's salary. In the fifteen years since, the value of the house had doubled as the real estate market boomed. In the fifteen years since, Clarissa had gone, his five-year-old boy was now a twenty-year-old Ecstasy-popper on seizure medication, and the cop's salary had given way to other forms of support. Clarissa and the kid had picked up and moved to Warminster; Saugherty kept the house out of sheer inertia. He kept meaning to rent a place closer to the city where he did most of his work, but never got around to it.

But as he sat on his back lawn in the spring air and watched his $135,000 (current market value) twin burn, Saugherty thought about none of this. Instead, his mind was still trying to wrap around something else.

No, not the fact that his former confidant and best friend, Earl Mothers, was a burnt piece of North Philly brisket inside his smoldering garage.

No, not the fact that three other heavily armed guys—sounded like Junior Black Mafia—were also in the Colony Drive BBQ pit.

Nor the fact that Saugherty, sooner or later, was going to have to come up with a story to explain his dead friend and dead niggers inside his burning home.

It was the mute.

He spoke.

All this time, the guy could talk. He'd been fooling people for months, maybe years. Saugherty didn't know how old the info on the I.O. was, but it wasn't as if the mute detail cropped up yesterday. Patrick Selway Lennon had been fooling people for a long time. It probably made him attractive as a getaway driver—what better accomplice than one who can't sing to the cops?

Even when it came down to it, when his life was on the line and any other person would have been pleading for it, the guy kept quiet.

Then why did he bother with that final spoken jab? Irish brogue and everything?

Remove this, *ya fuckin' arseholes.*

An anger limit. The guy had a boiling point, and the lid had blown off the pot just then. This would be useful.

Now Saugherty had to find the guy. He assumed he'd survived the blast, just as Saugherty had. That door had probably shielded him. Saugherty had barely cleared the garage door leading into the basement when the tank went up. When he saw the aim line, from gun to tank, Saugherty decided to screw the charade. He jumped up and ran for it. Two of the four guys—including Mothers—spun their heads around to watch Saugherty run. The others were focused on Lennon, and that gun poking out from beneath the door. Within seconds, the room was full of fire, and Saugherty was diving behind a love seat. A fireball whipped through the air above him, and everything in his basement went up. He had to hurl a chair through the basement bay window to make it out to the lawn.

Lennon hadn't come out that way. Saugherty had sat there on his lawn, holding his pistol, waiting for him.

He must have gone out the front.

Saugherty walked around the side of the house toward the street. His next-door neighbor, a Home Depot manager named Jimmy Hadder, grabbed him by the arm. "Jesus, are you okay?"

"Home invasion," muttered Saugherty. "Bunch of black guys knocked me out, robbed me, set the place on fire." He was spinning off the top of his head. He realized he should stop before he talked himself into a corner he couldn't explain later. "One guy got out—you see him, Jim?"

"Yeah—he went up toward Axe Factory. But he looked white."

"You never can tell these days. Thanks, Jimbo."

Axe Factory Road, which Colony Drive spilled into. From there, it was two choices: east or west. Saugherty thanked him and started jogging toward the end of the cul-de-sac.

Down toward the park: nada. Up toward Welsh Road: a glimpse of his guy, turning a corner.

Got you.

Saugherty ran back for the car he'd taken from Lennon, then realized it had been parked in the garage.

Convenience

LENNON STOLE A HUNTER GREEN 1997 CHEVY CAVALIER parked on the side of a street named Tolbut. Now a Chevy: that was easy pickings. He'd learned how to hot-wire a car on a Chevy. Plus, no alarm, and the Club attached to the steering wheel wasn't locked. People never locked them. But what made the car even more attractive was the sweatshirt rolled up in a ball in the backseat. Lennon drove two blocks, pulled over, removed his bloodied, ripped sweatshirt, and put on the new one. It was emblazoned with the words Father Judge High School. He'd regressed from college to high school overnight.

A few turns, and he found himself on what looked like a main drag—Welsh Road. Ten minutes up the road, across from a main artery road, Roosevelt Boulevard, was a 7-Eleven. Lennon pulled in and entered the store. His shoulder ached; his skin burned. And Saugherty was right. He was beginning to smell a little ripe. When he put some miles between himself and that burning house, he'd have to do a little rudimentary first aid. Even if that just meant dumping some vodka over it, slapping a bandage on it.

The occupant of room 219 hadn't kept any money lying around; college kids never did. So Lennon had to pull a little stickup. He was loathe to do it, since it was just the kind of thing to attract attention to himself. But the prepaid calling cards were behind the counter, and there was no easy way to do the five-finger discount.

Besides, he could use a little dough to hold him over until he reached the money in the car. And compared to the murders he'd just racked up, a 7-Eleven heist wasn't shit.

Lennon selected a detailed map of Philadelphia streets from a spinner rack. He had a better fix on where he was when he crossed Roosevelt Boulevard, but a quick glance at the map confirmed it. He was up in Northeast Philadelphia, about twenty-five minutes away from downtown. Saugherty had taken him home. From the looks of the map, the quickest way back down was to take the boulevard, also known as Route 1, down to where it merged with I-76 headed into downtown. He replaced the map on the spinner rack.

He picked up a copy of the *Philadelphia Daily News*, a packet of precooked chicken strips—easy protein—and a bottle of water. As an afterthought, he grabbed a chunky white stick of Old Spice deodorant. He placed them on the counter.

The counter kid looked at him funny as he bagged the stuff.

Chances were, he attended Father Judge High School. Lennon picked up the bottom of the sweatshirt and showed him the Glock tucked into the waist of his jeans. He pointed to the cash register, and then to the bag. The kid understood. He opened the register, scooped out bills, and shoved them in the bag. Next, Lennon pointed to the prepaid calling cards.

"How many?" the kid asked.

Lennon just curled his fingers into his hand. *Give them to me.*

"Okay." The kid grabbed a stack and slid them into the bag.

Lennon took the bag.

"See you in class," he said, smirking. From the looks of it, the kid looked completely thrilled. Lennon had probably just fulfilled a long-term work fantasy/running gag. *Dude, I was totally robbed!*

There was a security camera in the place, but at this point, Lennon reasoned, it was beside the point.

After fifteen minutes on Roosevelt Boulevard, Lennon fought his way to the outer lanes and turned into a large mall parking lot. He found a pay phone bank inside a Strawbridge's department store and used one of the prepaid calling cards to dial Katie's disposable cell phone. The emergency one.

Prepaid calling cards were the best thing to happen to planning heists since the invention of the road map. Absolutely untraceable—these rip-off companies bought long-distance minutes in bulk and sold them to people too poor to have home phones or with shitty enough credit to be turned down by long-distance phone companies or criminals who didn't want their calls traced. There were no bargains to be had, even though the cards claimed significant savings per minute. But when you used a prepaid card to call a cell phone that would only be used once, then tossed away, you had a next-to-perfectly secure means of communication.

Katie's disposable rang five times, and then an automated voice-mail message picked up.

Incoming

KATIE'S CELL PHONE CHIRPED. SHIT. SHE COULDN'T stop to pick it up now. Not with the business end of a Beretta in this Russian gangster's mouth.

Wait.

Only two people had this disposable number. One of them was Patrick. Which would make it pointless to continue negotiations with this tight-lipped Russian prick.

"Hold on a second, okay? Of course you will." Katie fumbled in her bag, found the phone, and flicked it open one-handed, but it was too late. The call was gone. Fuck.

She removed the gun from the guy's mouth and then proceeded to pistol-whip him into unconsciousness. He wasn't going to help, anyway. Claimed he knew nothing. Katie dialed in to check her messages, wiping the pistol clean on the guy's sofa.

The Russian hadn't been difficult to find. Henry refused to name names, and begged her to come over to his apartment to think things through. But eventually, he relented, and gave her one: Evsei Fieuchevsky. "I don't know that he's involved, but he might know some people who might know."

Fieuchevsky had claimed to know nothing, and it didn't matter. A search of his desk drawer revealed an old-fashioned address book. Somebody down the line would know what had happened to Patrick.

Outgoing

LENNON DIDN'T LEAVE A MESSAGE. HE NEVER DID—IT wasn't worth it. He'd just try later. He tried not to read too much into the fact that Katie didn't pick up their emergency line. He was the only one who had the number. Either she was showering, or temporarily away from her phone. Or she expected him to be dead. And now she knew he was alive.

No time to think about it now.

On to the next item on the agenda.

He was very anxious to leave Philadelphia.

Manhunt

SAUGHERTY WATCHED LENNON USE THE PHONES. THE guy didn't move his mouth at all. Was he retrieving a message, or listening to instructions? Saugherty almost wished he were a cop again. He could put someone on the Strawbridge's phones, try to get a fix on the call. But he was a loner. Working this solo. In a car—a royal blue Kia—borrowed from his neighbor Jimmy.

Calling Mothers had been the mistake of the year. He wasn't going to repeat that mistake.

He was going to follow Lennon to the money, then pop Lennon and take the money. Call a tip in to the FBI. Let them pick up their man, deal with the mess. Saugherty would still need a story, but that could come later.

Lennon left Strawbridge's, but didn't return to his stolen car. He simply strolled the length of the store, on the side away from the main bustle of the mall, and selected another vehicle—some early model Chevy. He was inside within seconds. Saugherty couldn't even see how he did it. Amazing. It reminded him of a video game his son loved called *Grand Theft Auto III.* "You'll dig this, Dad," his kid had said, but the game appalled Saugherty. It was all about a guy who went around carjacking and heisting and killing; your score was measured in dollars you either stole or earned via underworld activity. According to his son, it was also a badge of honor to rack up as many "wanted" stars as you could— the maximum was six—and the easiest way to do that was kill cops. His son loved this game. It apparently didn't dawn on him that his father used to earn their daily bread putting his life on the line as a cop, facing off against real-life scumbags who also considered it a badge of honor to snuff a pig.

Anyway, the protagonist of the game had no trouble at all stealing cars, parked or otherwise occupied. You simply moved your man close to the car, then pressed the button. This guy, it was like he was pressing that button. Boom. He was in the car.

Saugherty followed him out of the parking lot and back onto Roosevelt Boulevard.

He wished he'd had more time to read up on this guy. Everyone underestimated Saugherty, and Saugherty kept underestimating the fake mute.

What was his story? Where were his two partners, and why weren't they sitting on the money? Or were they? And Lennon was fighting to collect his third?

No. Something had gone wrong. Pro heisters never hung around the target city. They struck hard, struck fast, and got the hell out. There was a wrinkle somewhere, which kept Lennon here.

But what was the wrinkle?

Damn it, Saugherty. Before you started pickling your brains on a daily basis, you were a pretty good investigator. Figure it out. Keep thinking ahead. This could be the difference between the life you've always wanted to lead and life in a (now) burned-up twin over in Pennypack Park.

The dash clock in his neighbor's car read 9:34 A.M. He hadn't been up this early in years.

Had he been up all night? He had.

Lennon followed Roosevelt Boulevard all the way down, through lower Northeast Philly and past crappy areas like Logan and Hunting Park and Feltonville and other neighborhoods that had been vibrant at some distant point in the past—full of factories and jobs and neighborhood delicatessens and candy shops and people who swept their front stoops every day. Now they rotted. Some people still tried to believe the neighborhoods were worth saving. You could see them every now and again, along the boulevard. A house with a new paint job and crisp awning. But the problem was, it was usually right next to a gaping hole in the row where Licenses & Inspections had finally ordered a home's destruction. Nobody wanted to move into places like these anymore—certainly not anybody who could potentially save a neighborhood.

Saugherty wondered what Lennon thought of the view—if he noticed it at all. According to the guy's I.O., he had been born in Listowel, Ireland, but who knows where he had spent his formative years. Maybe it was here. Maybe he grew up in a shithole like Feltonville, and pulled jobs to ensure that he'd never have to live in a shithole ever again.

If so, it was a reason Saugherty could understand. He'd done the same thing. Hell, it was why he was doing this now.

The boulevard trimmed itself down from twelve lanes to four—two in each direction. Lennon kept driving. He passed the sign marked KELLY DRIVE. Up ahead, the boulevard ended and offered two choices: I-76 West, into the suburbs, and I-76 East, which swung past downtown Philly, then South Philly, then finally the Philly International Airport. There was nothing for Lennon out west—unless he had a hankering to see Valley Forge, where George Washington and his posse wrapped their bleeding feet in rags and prepared to duke it out with the British.

No, Lennon headed east. Big surprise. The question now was: downtown Philly, near the scene of the crime, or right to the airport and up and out of here?

Well, Lennon wasn't headed out of town on what he had on him, unless he had stashed a getaway bag in an airport locker. Saugherty had given him a thorough field stripping, and the guy didn't have a dime on him. His little convenience store stickup couldn't have netted him more than fifty dollars. Read the signs on the door. They're telling the truth. Yeah, the only thing he stole from that 7-Eleven, as far as Saugherty could tell, was a bunch of calling cards and beef jerky.

Breakfast of champions. Although Saugherty wouldn't have passed up a few sticks of beef right now. He was starving—the last thing he'd eaten were those fucking Memphis Dogs.

As predicted, Lennon took an exit that spat him out downtown. Saugherty almost lost him—Lennon took another sudden exit on the right, to Twenty-third Street.

Damn. The guy *was* returning to the scene of the crime.

The Bitter Taste of Blood

EVSEI FIEUCHEVSKY WAS NOT HAVING A GOOD MORNING. First, the news of his son. Involved with bank robbers, and now dead? How could his son do this? What had Mikal been thinking? Then the embarrassing mistake with the daughter of the fat Italian. Then finally, the arrival of the crazy bitch with a pistol, breaking into his home in Morrell Park and threatening his life unless he told her what they did with the bank robber.

The bank robber who had probably murdered his son.

Thank God his Dimitra wasn't alive to see his shame.

During the assault, Fieuchevsky had merely held his tongue. He had decided to show patience with the crazy bitch. Let her rant and rave and spit and threaten. It did not matter. Soon, his employees—the ones who found Mikal's truck—would arrive. Within thirty minutes, the crazy bitch would be dangling from the end of a meat hook in his garage, begging for a merciful conclusion to the proceedings.

But then the bitch actually paused to answer her cell phone, and without warning, beat Fieuchevsky into unconsciousness.

This was madness.

Madness, too, that his tan Naugahyde couch was streaked with his own blood. The crazy bitch had beaten him about the face, then wiped the blood clean on his furniture. His $4,000 set. Like it was Kleenex.

Fieuchevsky couldn't decide who he'd enjoy seeing tortured more—the bank robber, or his crazy bitch.

He'd savor both.

Then, a name popped into his head. An outsider, who knew this sort of thing. A friend his son had once mentioned. "This finance guy I met, Dad? He used to rob banks. Just keep that bit on the Q.T.—he don't like anybody knowing."

Fieuchevsky picked up the phone.

Prelude

LENNON PARKED ON ARCH STREET, TWO BLOCKS AWAY from the lot. This Chevy sucked—he was glad to be ditching it. It could stay in Philadelphia and the two could rot together. From what he'd seen on the drive down, the city was already halfway there.

Call him bitter.

The moment he saw the Honda Prelude he could breathe again. Not that he was worried he wouldn't—the only other two people who knew about the location and make and model of the car were both dead, decomposing in a tube down by the river. No, it was about reassurance on a cosmic level. That everything he touched didn't necessarily have to turn to shit.

His shoulder was really worrying him now. It smelled funny, like Chinese food left on a kitchen counter too long. That meant infection. That meant trouble, unless he found a doctor who could prescribe antibiotics soon. The wound had pretty much closed and caked on itself; his shoulder would never be perfect, but at least he wasn't bleeding out. On his personal pyramid of woes, the shoulder was the apex. That was followed by existential worries, of double crosses and bad luck and everything else mental. Below that was a thick base of bruises and contusions and cuts and sprains and everything else. Lennon had a feeling that if you were to remove every broken/ailing part of his body, all he'd have left would be two eyeballs and a spleen. Maybe not even the spleen.

But everything would heal. Money would help. Money and a plane ticket and a room at a resort hotel and a friendly doctor and good food and rest and music. That was it. And still a half a million left to live on. Spent frugally, that money could last Lennon until he was forty years old. Katie, too.

If Katie was still in the picture.

Lennon turned the corner, spied the lot. There was an attendant in the booth, but he was too engrossed in something perched in his lap. Not many cars were parked here on a Saturday morning, despite this being a long-term lot. This vaguely worried Lennon. He'd imagined more cars, burying the Prelude in a sea of pricier, sleeker cars with a higher street value.

He walked down the second row, where they'd left it. Nothing yet. It was probably down farther.

The row ended. Nothing.

Had to be the third row.

Halfway down the third row, the attendant took an interest in Lennon.

Lennon pressed two fingers to his neck, feeling for the carotid artery.

Steady now.

Steady.

On.

an Interlude in Nausea

KATIE THOUGHT BACK ON HER VISIT TO MORRELL PARK. It could have been handled better. Michael would definitely *not* have approved. Neither would Patrick.

Then again, Patrick was probably no longer alive, so what did it matter?

Unless that was him calling. And he was hiding out somewhere.

There was only one way to find out. Katie pulled her rented car over to the side of Grant Avenue and dialed Henry. On her public cell, not the emergency one. Her stomach did flip-flops, but she kept it together by breathing oxygen. Oxygen dispelled the nausea, if she tried hard enough.

"Hello?"

"Did you call me about twenty minutes ago?"

"No. But wait—don't go. Let me get rid of this other line."

Click.

Shit. Katie didn't know what she was hoping to hear. That Henry had called, or that he hadn't. If he really hadn't, Patrick was somewhere. But then why didn't he leave a message?

Because the stubborn bastard never left a message. It was against his religion.

Katie felt her stomach roil again, and she concentrated on breathing.

The line clicked back.

"Katie, where are you?"

She ignored the question. "Someone called me twenty minutes ago. On the other line. Only two people have that number. You and Patrick."

"So then he's fine. Tell me where you are, and I'll send a car for you."

"No. Help me think. Where would Patrick be?"

"I'm no good thinking over the phone," he said. "You know that."

"What good are you at all?"

Damnit, Patrick. Call again. Let me know what's going on. Tell me I just didn't pistol-whip a Russian gangster for no good reason.

"Look, girlie. I've had enough abuse for one morning. You know where I am. You want me to help you figure this out, stop by. And let me just add that since you've gotten knocked up, you've been nothing but moody."

"Fuck you," Katie said.

The line was silent.

"I'll see you in twenty minutes," she added.

The Outsider Pays Off

HENRY WILCOXSON CLICKED BACK TO THE OTHER line. "Evsei? Thanks for waiting. I think I can help you after all."

Void

LENNON FELT A TAP ON HIS SHOULDER. IT WAS THE parking attendant.

"Can I help you?" he said, but his tone was just the opposite. *Can I get rid of you quick, so I can go back to my booth?*

Lennon shook his head. But the attendant persisted.

"What kind of car you looking for?"

Lennon ignored him and scanned the last row of cars, near the edge of the lot. He knew they hadn't parked the Prelude here, but maybe some parking attendant moved the cars around somehow. They did that sometimes, especially to clear a street for a work crew; they just loaded the cars on flatbeds and moved them where they wanted. Although that seemed highly unlikely, Lennon searched anyway.

The attendant seemed to give up, and walked back to his booth. He kept giving Lennon strange looks.

Fuck him. Where the hell was the car?

Only two possibilities.

One—and this was another highly unlikely event—somebody decided to boost the Honda Prelude, and got a nice surprise when they looked in the trunk. In this case, Holden would have been correct to be nervous, and the fates were working against them all.

That was bullshit.

The more likely possibility was that one of his partners, Bling or Holden, had double-crossed him. Of course, that brought up two additional possibilities: one, the betrayer was either working with the Russians, in which case he knew the battering van was coming, and braced himself for impact, then led them to the Prelude. Two, the betrayer survived the Russian ambush just as Lennon had, but beat him to the Prelude and sped away, assuming the others were dead. Lennon hadn't rushed back to the Prelude, thinking it was better to heal first and let the heat die down.

But now he saw that hesitation was just one of a long series of mistakes he'd made in the past twenty-four hours. If Lennon had gone right for the Prelude, that Saugherty prick wouldn't have caught him napping on Kelly Drive, and he would have only two deaths on his tab, instead of at least . . . how many was it? Two, three (Saugherty), four (his big friend), five, six, seven strangers with guns? For a decidedly nonviolent heister, Lennon had racked up an uncomfortably large body count.

Sort it out later. Solve the problem now.

"Dude."

It was the parking attendant again.

"Phone. It's for you."

He held out a cell phone.

I.P.B.

THE MOMENT RAY "CHARDONNAY" PERELLI LEFT THE Dining Car, he called his lawyer, Donovan Platt.

"How do I find somebody?"

"It would help if you could be a little more specific, Ray."

"I need to find a bank robber."

"A specific one, or any old bank robber?"

"Specific one."

Pause. "This guy do the Wachovia job yesterday?"

"Yeah."

Platt whistled. "What, are you trying to earn your Boy Scout merit badge thirty years too late?"

"Fuck you, you bagadonuts."

"Hey, calm down. You know what—*don't* tell me why. Who am

I to ask why, right? You want to find this guy, try the usual places."

"Like where?"

"These pro heist guys are predictable. If he's still in the city, it's because the money is still in the city. Try long-term parking lots, bus station lockers, storage joints. If he's trying to get out of the city, he'll be at the airport—which makes him a bit easier to track—or driving, which makes it impossible. While these guys are predictable, they're not easy to track down. The whole point is to blend into the background and slip out as quickly as possible."

"Wait, wait. Parking lots, bus stations, you said?"

"Yeah, Ray. Anyplace where you can hide stuff without raising eyebrows."

"Okay. Thanks, Don."

"Can I ask . . . geez, should I even ask?"

"Ask what?"

"Ask what you need a bank robber for."

"Don't ask, Don. Catch ya later."

The Italian mob in Philadelphia was dealt a series of death blows in the early 1980s, but hung on through that decade and most of the decade after. Then right before 9/11, a blistering series of federal indictments destroyed the remaining leadership.

Within months, nine players and associates were shipped off to various federal lockups across the country to eat shitty food and work menial jobs that paid thirty-five cents an hour.

Within a few years, all that remained of the Philly mob was a motley collection of mid-level capos who wanted to rule what remained and small-time hoods who fancied themselves gangsters. They had the suits, but none of the muscle to fill them out. They had the small-time scams, but none of the brains to make them mean anything.

All that remained of the Philadelphia mob, actually, was a fairly efficient communication system, older and more secure than Ma Bell. The old guys, the new guys, the mid-level guys, they all talked. That's all there was to do. Talk.

So when Ray Perelli decided to put out an APB on the bank robber the Russians wanted so badly, it didn't take long for the word to get out. Especially because it involved the Russians. And shoving it up their vodka-drinking asses.

Within fifty minutes, Perelli received word that a strange guy was poking around a long-term parking lot down beneath the JFK overpass near Twenty-second Street. Perelli called the attendant, who was a cousin of a friend of his next-door neighbor, working his way through his sophomore year at Tyler Art School. What tipped the attendant off was the fact that the guy didn't talk—didn't the heister lose his voice? Perelli promised the guy next semester's art books if he could keep the guy there in the lot. "How am I supposed to do that?" the attendant asked.

Jesus, Perelli thought. Kids don't want to work for shit these days. "Put him on the phone," he said.

Which is how Perelli found the bank robber that the Russians couldn't. The Russians didn't know the city. They hadn't been here long enough.

Fuck those Russians, Perelli thought. Fuck them up their stupid asses.

Let's Have a Drink

HEY THERE."

Lennon listened.

"You're the guy I'm looking for, aren't you? The bank heister?"

Lennon listened.

"Now I know you can't answer. Poster says you're a mute. So what we're going to do is this. You listen up, and then hand the phone back to my guy there. If you agree, nod your head and he'll tell me. Okay? If not, just don't do anything, and he'll tell me that."

The attendant looked bored.

Lennon listened. What the hell was this about, anyway? This wasn't the Russian mob. At least he didn't think it was the Russian mob. The Russians would be more pissed. The guy sounded too casual. Too relaxed. Was this an associate of the big cop?

"Okay. Here's what I'm offering. I've got what you're looking for. You let my guy there drive you out to see me, we'll talk, and see what we can work out."

Lennon thought about this and quickly decided that it didn't make sense. He was looking for a Honda Prelude with $650,000 in the trunk. If the guy on the line had the car and the money, why would he be trying to work out a deal? No, he was offering something else.

"All I want is a little conversation. I'll get you some medical attention, too—my guys say you look pretty fucked up. Get you a glass of wine, some good food, and you listen to my proposal. You don't like it, you walk right out. I'm being straight with ya. Whaddya think?"

Lennon knew this was bullshit, but he didn't have much choice. He was standing in a parking lot with no Honda Prelude, and no $650,000. He had nowhere to go, except a prison or a Russian *mafiya* torture chamber or that steel pipe down by the river. He wasn't about to flee town screaming yet. Not without that money. There was the off chance that this dipshit knew something. And he had to know *something,* because he knew where to find Lennon.

"Okay. If it's a yes, you mind handing the phone back to my guy?"

Lennon gave the phone back.

The guy on the other end said something.

"Uh, no."

Something else.

"No, man, I don't carry that shit."

And something else.

"Mace, man. That's it. I got some Mace."

Jesus Christ, Lennon thought. How was it that, all of a sudden, his dim future seemed to lie in the hands of a Philly gangster on the phone and one desperately retarded man? Not that there was much difference between the two.

Lennon tapped the guy on the shoulder.

"Hold on," the guy said.

Lennon lifted his Father Judge sweatshirt.

"Oh shit," the guy said. "This guy is packing. Seriously. Like . . . oh man. What the fuck am I supposed . . . Hold on. He wants to go. So we're like, going. See you in a few. Wait, wait, wait. Where do you live again?"

Power

100

Party

THERE WAS A SMALL KNOCK. BEFORE WILCOXSON could stand, Fieuchevsky was up and answering the door.

Katie's face appeared in the doorway. She registered surprise when she saw Fieuchevsky, even more so when the Russian punched her in the face. Katie's body flopped against the wall, then slid sideways down to the carpet. Fieuchevsky slammed the door shut, then grabbed Katie by the wrists and dragged her into the living room.

"Jesus, Evsei. What are you doing?"

"This bitch pistol-whipped me in my own home. I'm giving her a taste."

"You can't do that."

Fieuchevsky looked at Wilcoxson. "Oh, I can't?"

"She's pregnant," Wilcoxson said. "A fall like that, she could lose the baby." Not that Wilcoxson really cared, one way or the other.

"Fuck her. She pistol-whipped me. And her husband killed my son. You think I give a shit about her baby?"

"She's not married. Besides, you don't want her. You want Lennon."

"I want their entire families dead."

Crazy Russian bastard. Wilcoxson looked at Katie, sprawled on his carpet, blood streaming from her nose. Even unconscious, she looked beautiful.

Wilcoxson had been in love with her since the first day Lennon had introduced them. Lennon had called her his "sister," but

Wilcoxson knew better. He'd met plenty of heisters over the years who had introduced him to many "sisters."

He had never met anyone like Katie before. Her smile set his soul at ease. She was shorter than he preferred. Her hair was a dirty reddish-brown, a far cry from the blondes he'd enjoyed over the years. And her body wasn't quite the proportions he usually desired—thin, wide, thin, then wider. But somehow, Katie managed to look perfect.

From the beginning, this had all been about Katie. Wilcoxson had mentored Lennon—come to think of him as something of a son—though he'd never wanted children, and still didn't. Still, it had been nice to be able to brag about some of the jobs he'd pulled over the years. Lennon was a quick study, and loved to listen. What else could he do? Wilcoxson had recommended him to a few teams here and there, and the kid had worked out well as a wheelman.

But from the day Lennon brought Katie by to meet Wilcoxson, everything changed. He knew it'd just be a matter of time before he could take her off Lennon's hands. Lennon was making decent coin, but he really didn't have all that much to offer her. Not compared to what Wilcoxson had glommed over the years. He could give her the life she deserved. And frankly, Wilcoxson deserved a young woman like Katie. He had experienced enough of the chase, the drama. He wanted to take Katie and settle down. Or at least give it a run.

A few weeks ago, Katie had called him. Confided in him. Asked him what Lennon would think. She didn't want to tell him right away; he was in the middle of planning a job in Philadelphia, and she never liked to disturb him while his brain was embroiled in a job. Wilcoxson invited Katie to dinner, and they spoke warmly, Katie confiding in Wilcoxson like a daughter would confide in her father. (Her own father, a minor armed robber, had been killed in a shoot-out in 1978.)

But as much as Wilcoxson loved that she trusted him implicitly, his heart sank.

A child.

A child would tie her to Lennon, at least for the foreseeable future.

That night, he decided that Lennon would have to be eliminated.

Around the same time, Wilcoxson had made the acquaintance of an ambitious young musician named Mikal Fieuchevsky, who also happened to be the son of a Russian *mafiya vor.* It was at a December "Power 100" party thrown by a local magazine, and Mikal had approached him about fund-raising. (For all the movers and shakers in the city knew, Wilcoxson was a moderately successful "financial consultant.") Mikal was trying to complete his first album, and although his father had kicked in some money, it was nowhere near enough to do the project the way Mikal had wanted. Mikal wanted name producers, top-shelf recording gear and session players. This was going to be his statement, Mikal said, his eyes wide. No more South Jersey dives and resorts; he was going to break out huge like Springsteen or Bon Jovi, but with a modern sound. Blues, hip-hop, electronica, he went on, with Wilcoxson only half-listening. He wasn't much of a music fan.

But later, when Katie came to him and the Lennon problem emerged, and he thought back on Mikal's need for money, and a connection was made.

That was what Wilcoxson did best. Make connections. He'd always believed that genius was measured by the connections you could make, either in terms of information or people or financial assets.

Wilcoxson decided to sell out Lennon's job to Mikal.

During phone calls over the next week, Wilcoxson pried small details out of Katie, and they were enough to piece together the heist. A small article in the *Philadelphia Inquirer* clinched it—a large amount of cash was going to be delivered to the Wachovia Bank at Seventeenth and Market in October. From there, Wilcoxson was able to figure out exactly what Lennon planned to do.

(After all, he'd taught him how to do it.) He also fingered Lennon's partners. Only a handful of pros were working the Philly scene. He approached the likely candidate, and that candidate agreed to betray his partners.

Wilcoxson told Mikal to tell his team where to be, and boom, they'd be $650,000 richer. Minus Wilcoxson's $65,000 fee, of course. Mikal was more than happy to agree to the conditions of the deal, which included the removal of the bank robbers from the face of the earth.

Exit Patrick Selway Lennon.

Enter Wilcoxson, to pick up the pieces. He would deal with a baby just fine, if it meant having Katie. But if it were to disappear like its father, that would be just as well.

Wilcoxson watched her on the floor, bleeding.

Now to calm the crazy Russian asshole. He didn't feel bad about Mikal getting snuffed—hey, the guy didn't follow through on his end of the deal. The young Russian had let one of the bank robbers live, and if it was Lennon, there was more work to be done.

Besides, there was $650,000 out there waiting to be claimed.

Saturday P.M.

Here's our credentials.
— HARRY PIERPONT, MEMBER OF THE DILLINGER
GANG, SHOWING A PRISON WARDEN A GUN

Smell the Roses

RAY PERELLI WAS PLEASED WITH HIMSELF. WITH ONLY word of mouth and a quick phone conversation, this bank robber guy was coming to *him*. Russian pricks were looking all over the city for him, and nothing. Perelli had him. Or was going to have him, in a manner of minutes.

Now. What the hell was he going to *do* with him?

Perelli had told the bank robber, "I've got what you're looking for." He knew the guy had to be looking for something. Otherwise, he would have lammed out of here long ago. Was it money from a recent heist? Is that what the Russians were holding over his head? Nah. Couldn't be. Smart bank robber wouldn't hang around for that, would he? What were the odds of recovering money from the Reds? Something else. C'mon, Ray, let's pull an answer out of our ass.

After ninety seconds of deep thought, Perelli decided to make a phone call.

"Hello?"

"Hey, yeah, Evsei?" Perelli pronounced it *evsee*. This was not the correct pronunciation.

"Who is this?"

"Ray Perelli."

"Who?"

Perelli wanted to say, *Hey, fuck you, you vodka-slurping Russian cocksucker.* But this was an information-gathering phone call. Insults would get him nowhere.

"We had breakfast, just a little while ago."

"Oh, yes, Mr. Perelli. Forgive me. I've been distracted, this business with my son."

"Hey, don't worry about it. I can only imagine."

"What do you want?"

"I seem to have somebody you're looking for."

"What did you say?"

"That bank robber guy. One of my men rounded him up. I'm going to be seeing him soon."

A pause.

"That is very good news, Mr. Perelli. I cannot tell you how much this pleases me."

"Yeah, it's great. Only problem is, I need a little something from you."

"Ahhh," the Russian said. "Cash."

"No," said Perelli, insulted for the second time this morning. "Just some info. See, I lured this guy here under what you might call false pretenses. I told him I had something he wanted. Only, I don't know what he wants. Can you tell me?"

The Russian chuckled. "Oh, I have something he wants."

"What's that?"

"His pregnant girlfriend. You tell the bank robber I have a loaded gun to his girlfriend's belly."

Jesus Christ, Perelli thought. These Red bastards don't fuck around.

"I guess that'll work," he said quietly. "But how do I prove it to him?"

"Hmmm. Hold on a minute."

Perelli held. He had waved off the cash thing, but only temporarily. Yeah, this thing was going to come down to cash. He wanted to see how far the Russian prick would go, how high a price he would affix to the forehead of his son's murderer. It wasn't going to be $650, Perelli knew that much.

"Okay. I have something. If the bank robber doesn't believe you, tell him, 'Smell the roses.'"

"Say what?"

"It will mean something to him. Between him and his girl-friend."

"How do you know that?"

"I've got a source here."

Weird. But Evsei had no reason to lie about this. It would give Perelli something to work with.

"Great. And since you brought it up, what kind of price is on this guy's head, anyway?"

"We can discuss that later."

"Yeah. Well, you see, I kind of wanted to get that ironed out now."

"When I see the bank robber, you will be amply rewarded."

Amply. What the fuck did "amply" mean? What, was he going to kick in another $650?

Hose Down the White Tile

SAUGHERTY FOLLOWED LENNON AND THE PARKING GUY all the way down Broad Street into the depths of South Philadelphia. Saugherty noticed that Lennon had pulled a gun—the very Glock 19 he'd given him early this morning—on the parking attendant before they climbed into the car, and he could only assume that it was pointed at the guy the entire ride. Despite this, he obeyed all traffic laws, which was impressive, considering.

They pulled up to Ninth and Catherine, near a one-hundred-year-old South Philly restaurant called Dominick's Little Italy. The place was very familiar to Saugherty. Famous for 1960s-era gangland powwows and grisly 1980s-era gangland hits, Dominick's also served up some amazing Italian food. Saugherty had taken his ex-wife here for their fifth anniversary. He had enjoyed pointing out the local capos and wannabes sitting at each table. His wife had been too nervous to enjoy herself. "Will you stop pointing," she'd hushed him, under her breath.

The thing that stuck most in his memory about Dominick's Little Italy: all the white tile. It was everywhere—the floor, the walls . . . maybe even the ceiling, for all he remembered. White tile, bordered by black tiles. The main dining room looked like one big high school shower. Saugherty joked at the time that the white tiles just made it easier to hose down the blood after a mob hit. His ex didn't think that was funny, either.

What was Lennon doing down here? Was he forcing the parking attendant to buy him a plate of raviolis?

There was a small dive bar catty-corner to Dominick's. Saugherty parked the car. He was relieved to find that it was one of those old-man bars he loved—no fancy bar menu, no karaoke, no microbrews. Just wood paneling and two beers on tap. Coasters were about the fanciest thing in the joint. Squared white tile covered the floor. The ceiling was stamped tin, painted over. The stool seats were covered with puffy vinyl, and there were peanuts in black plastic bowls on the bar top. Best of all, there was a huge greasy window, partially obscured by a set of 1950s-era blinds, that gave Saugherty a front and side view of Ralph's. When Lennon left the premises, Saugherty would know about it.

Which left only one thing to do: order a fucking drink already.

Saugherty asked for a boilermaker—a shot of whiskey dropped into a mug of beer. The bartender didn't ask what kind of whiskey, what kind of beer. Saugherty liked that. The glass sank and tapped the bottom of the mug with a dull thud, like two submarines tapping each other underwater. Saugherty downed it, then asked for a shot of Jack Daniel's and another beer. Jack and beer. That had been his drink of choice ten years ago, when shit with his ex had gotten out of control. He'd finish his shift, then head to the Ashton Tavern just down the road a piece from his house on Colony Drive.

The house that was burning.

Saugherty saluted it, and enjoyed the trip down memory lane. Every so often, he'd look across the street to see what was going on at Dominick's.

Two
Guns

LENNON WAS LED THROUGH THE RESTAURANT AND hallway and kitchen to a back office. A heavyset man wearing a crisp white button-down shirt was sitting behind an empty desk. This wasn't the man's usual desk. He was just borrowing it. "You're Lennon," he said. "I can tell by the face. Man, you look bad. Have a seat. You want something to drink? There's a pen and paper there. Write down what you want." The parking attendant left without a word.

Lennon sat down, but he didn't pick up the pen. He waited.

"Really. Go ahead. Anything you want. They've got a fully stocked bar here."

He picked up the pen and the legal pad beneath it. He scribbled a few words on the surface, then flipped the pad to show his host: *THE MONEY?*

The guy smiled. "I'll tell you right now, I don't have your money. Did I give you the impression I had your money? I don't think I did."

In some ways, this was a relief. The $650,000 was still out there somewhere. Lennon scribbled some more. He turned the pad over.

ICE WATER. CHICKEN BREAST.

"That's more like it. Get some food in your belly. If you don't mind me saying, I'm assuming you don't always look like a bum. Or smell like one."

The guy picked up a phone, punched in three buttons, said "Come here," then gave a teenaged boy in a white coat Lennon's order. The guy specified Boar's Head chicken breast, then turned his attention back to Lennon.

"You know, my daughter gave me a book last Christmas. What

the hell was it called? Something like *Outlaw Heroes of the 1930s.* Guys in there were Dillinger, Baby Face, Pretty Boy, the Barkers, Al Karpis, all those guys. I like how it was titled 'Heroes.' Ever see it?"

Lennon had. He was a voracious reader of true crime and history—that's how he had spent his wasted winter. Catching up on his reading, both crime stuff and a stack of science fiction novels. (Katie liked the sci-fi, too—Dick, Bester, Sturgeon—so they traded paperbacks back and forth at a feverish pace.) *Outlaw Heroes* was okay; nothing special. He remembered flipping through it on a lazy December afternoon. The guy clearly cribbed most of his stuff from other histories.

Lennon didn't write anything on the pad. He preferred to listen. Sooner or later, this guy was going to get to the point about Katie.

"Okay. Maybe you don't read much. You're busy. I'll get to the point. The Russian mob has your girlfriend. Intes Studios, down on Delaware Avenue. Suite 117."

Lennon stared at him. Girlfriend?

"I can tell by your look that you might doubt me. Well, they told me to tell you to smell the roses. That make any sense? That's supposed to be proof."

Fucking hell.

These bastards had Katie.

"Smell the roses" was one of their in-jokes from years ago. One Christmas, Lennnon found himself at one of Katie's girlfriend's houses for a holiday party. There was a big guy there. Named Joe. Joe was a bit of an idiot. Physical trainer from Florida. He spotted Lennon in a corner and took it upon himself to bring Lennon out of his shell. (Lennon was actually embroiled in a getaway plan, spinning the details and arrangements around in his head. He always did his best thinking in large groups, while nobody paid attention to him.) After a few awkward attempts at small talk, the guy grabbed Lennon by his shoulders and shook him. "C'mon, man, open up and live! You gotta smell the roses, dude!" From that point on, "smell the roses" had cropped up in countless conversations. It became shorthand for people who didn't understand The Life. It became shorthand for pretty much anybody who annoyed Katie and Lennon.

That meant Katie was here, in Philadelphia. And with some associates of the man behind this desk. Against her will, or perhaps otherwise. This didn't make sense yet.

Then again, nothing from the past twenty-four hours made sense.

The guy opened a desk drawer and pulled out a revolver. A black .38 with rubber handgrips. He popped open the chamber, placed it on the desk, then slid it across to Lennon. A box of bullets followed.

"They're expecting me to hand-deliver you," the guy said. "But I figure you can deliver yourself. Am I right?"

Lennon took the gun and bullets, waiting for the punch line. There had to be something else.

"Drink your ice water, eat your chicken, then go do what you have to. When it's done, feel free to come back here. I might have something else for you."

Lennon balanced the gun and box in his lap, then scribbled a hasty question. *YOUR PROPOSAL?*

The guy read it and smirked. "Nah, no proposal. I changed my mind."

Lennon stood up, gun and box in his hands.

"Don't you want to wait for your food? No, I guess you wouldn't. Tell you what. I'll have 'em save it for you. Come on back later. Bring your woman. We'll have dinner. Then we can talk. Maybe there's some business opportunities for you in Philadelphia."

Lennon left the office, but he still heard the guy talking behind him.

"Hey—you might want to use the back entrance. My guy said somebody followed you from the parking lot."

Preservation Mode

FOR CLOSE TO THIRTY MINUTES, WILCOXSON TAP-danced like a motherfucker. No, Evsei. Don't kill the girl. Killing the girl will do nothing. No, Evsei, trust me. Put her on my bed. She's better as bait, and Lennon will only go for it if she's alive. You want Lennon, remember? The guy who killed your son. The only way you're going to lure him out into the open is to use his girlfriend, and that only works if she's alive.

Evsei, the crazy fucker, wanted to gut Katie with a steak knife right there in the apartment, then dump both bodies in front of Lennon before hoisting him onto a meat hook. A regular family reunion. The Russian was absolutely blood crazy. No wonder young Mikal had been so eager to strike out on his own.

Wilcoxson needed Katie alive. That was the only thing that mattered. He also needed to figure out a way to let Evsei take his revenge on Lennon—a walking dead man, anyway—and extricate Katie and himself from the situation. And then allow both of them to take an extended vacation without having to worry about looking over his shoulder the whole time. Unlike the pathetic Italian mob, the Russian *mafiya* had tentacles.

But Wilcoxson also needed that $650,000 recovered. Fieuchevksy knew nothing about his son's plan to rob the bank robbers; in fact, he was still waiting for an explanation as to why his son was meeting with bank robbers in the first place.

So Wilcoxson whipped up a little speech.

"I made a few calls," he told the Russian. "Your son was not involved in that bank robbery."

Fieuchevsky's eyes closed and his lips tightened.

"He was approached by one of the robbers—this Patrick Lennon—who presented your son with an investment opportunity.

Lennon needed seed money to bankroll his next job, and your son gave him $10,000. In return, your son was promised six and a half times that amount—$65,000."

"But," Fieuchevsky started, "I gave him money."

"The important thing to remember is that your son, Mikal, approached this as a business deal. He didn't know he was dealing with a bank heister."

"What did he need the money for?"

"Your son is the victim here. Remember that."

"Didn't I give him enough?"

"Evsei," said Wilcoxson. "Listen to me. How would you like to kill this bank robber guy, and also make a lot of money in the process?"

This stopped the Mad Russian. He listened intently to Wilcoxson's plan—the details spinning out on the spot.

To Wilcoxson's surprise, he nodded.

"Good," Wilcoxson said. "Let me get the tape recorder."

Flagged

BY HIS THIRD BOILERMAKER, THE WORLD SEEMED TO make more sense. Sure, his house was burning . . . burnt . . . extinguished . . . but so what? That's why God made insurance. Saugherty watched Dominick's, looking for his boy, the bank robber. Sooner or later, he had to come back out the front. Sooner or later, he had to go for his $650,000. Sooner or later, Saugherty would get to finish the job he started late last night.

Somebody tapped him on the shoulder.

"Hey, buddy—what you lookin' at over there?"

Saugherty turned to face the guy standing to his right. The man was big and pasty, with oversized tortoiseshell glasses and a bushy black moustache.

Saugherty opened his mouth to speak, but he didn't have the chance to answer the question. A fist smashed his nose, and then another hit the back of his head as he slid off of the stool. Saugherty held up a hand to protest, but somebody grabbed it by the wrist, then snapped his forearm in half.

After that, he lost track of the fists and shoes.

a

Killing

in

the

Sun

THE CONVERTED WAREHOUSE SEEMED DESERTED—NO lights on in the windows, no cars in the small parking lot to the left. But Lennon knew the place had to be lousy with Russians. Especially after this morning. They were probably lined up, waiting to take turns. Russian brothers, friends, fathers. With guns. Knives. Probably chainsaws and rabid attack dogs, too.

And Katie.

How did they find her so quickly? Or put the two of them together, for that matter? Next to no one knew anything about

Lennon's family. Bling knew, but Bling was dead. The Russians had worked the network fast. That, or Katie had somehow heard the heist had gone wrong, and somehow figured out that the Russians were behind it, and went looking for payback, and now this. But that was a lot of somehows and maybes.

The other troubling possibility, of course, was that Katie was part of this whole setup, and was using herself as bait to lure Lennon out in the open so that he could be killed.

Either way, not cheery thoughts.

Neither was the fact that the Italian gangster back there had pretty much handed him a gun and told him to go kill a bunch of Russians. Likely, enemies in some Philadelphia turf war. Lennon didn't want to be in the middle of that shit.

Now, standing in the bright sun that baked Delaware Avenue, Lennon had nothing but these thoughts . . . and two loaded revolvers. If this were an action thriller, Lennon supposed he would also happen to be a master burglar, and would know how to sneak into virtually any building. But Lennon was not a burglar—he was a getaway driver. The studio looked huge, and probably had a dozen side entrances, but Lennon had no idea how to navigate any of them. He didn't know any Vietnam-style diversionary tactics.

Lennon pressed two fingers to his neck.

Ah, fuck it, he thought.

He pressed the buzzer next to the tag marked INTES STUDIOS.

The intercom crackled. "Yes?"

"Yo," Lennon said, in his best Philly accent. "We gotcher guy out heah."

"Yes, bring him in, please. Down the hall, to your right." There was a sharp buzz, and a lock mechanism opened.

Okay then.

Plastic signs directed Lennon through a lobby, down a slender hallway, to the right, and to another right. The doors marked INTES were already propped open with wooden shims. Inside was a lounge, and beyond that, a window-paneled recording studio.

Lennon had both guns in his hands and was ready to start blasting at will. But he wasn't ready for what awaited him inside the studio.

There was only one guy, standing inside a glass recording booth. A tall, swarthy man with gray hair slicked back on his thick skull, pointing a shotgun at him.

There was a tiny static pop, and a voice came over the speakers.

"Hello, Mr. Lennon."

It wasn't the guy standing there. The voice was distorted, warped. Its owner was nowhere in sight.

Lennon aimed his guns at the man in front of him anyway. Even though it was an awful shot, going through glass. These Russians probably planned it that way. He didn't have much of a chance of hitting him, not with shattering glass knocking his bullets out of line. And long before that, the man could easily pull his trigger and spray Lennon with a cone-shaped burst. Not to mention there were probably other gunmen hidden around the room, keeping their sights trained on him. It was a turkey shoot. Lennon was the turkey.

"We work for Evsei Fieuchevsky. His son, Mikal, is missing. You were one of the last people to see him."

That voice. Even with the distortion, Lennon could tell it wasn't Russian. The diction was too clean. It also had a nagging familiarity. Lennon recognized not the tone, but the way this guy put words together. He couldn't quite place it.

"Mr. Fieuchevsky has your girlfriend at another location. He very badly wants his son back."

Lennon darted his eyes around the studio, looking for a mirror that could be two-way. The speaker was watching him. Waiting for reactions.

"Before we discuss terms, Mr. Fieuchevksy would like to play something for you. A love song."

A what?

There was a click, a slight hiss over the speakers, and then a man coughing. "Okay," the voice, presumably on a tape, said. "'Life,' take five." A run of guitar notes, then silence, then loud strumming at a march tempo, almost like a funeral dirge. A minor chord. After two bars, a fuzzy bass and a muted drum machine kicked in. Then vocals:

> *I can see the writing on the wall*
> *When I hear you coming down the hall*
> *Have you finished all that you've begun?*
> *I can feel my life coming undone*

The song continued, but the volume dropped low, so that it played over the background.

"That song, 'Life Come Undone,' was written and performed by Mikal Fieuchevsky. It was one of many tracks from the album he had been recording during the past few weeks."

The song continued beneath the speaker's voice, almost as if a bizarre spoken-word segment had been appended to the middle of the recording.

"You see, Mr. Lennon, Mikal isn't just this man's son. He's the future of rock music. And you'd better pray to God he is alive and well."

Lennon stared at the quiet Russian through the glass. From the sound of that piece of shite, he thought, it's probably better he stays missing.

Living
Expenses

EVSEI HAD INSISTED ON THAT LAST BIT. PLAYING HIS son's lame-ass song. Wilcoxson had tried to explain that Lennon wouldn't give a shit, that Evsei should stick to the plan and make his demands as quickly as possible.

But the Mad Russian refused to bend. He had sent one of his guys into Intes Studios in the early morning hours to recover the unfinished digital recordings, and had spent some time listening through the rough tracks at home, crying and drinking Stoli and listening to portions again. This was my son, he'd said. That bank robber will hear what he destroyed. Evsei had tried to play some songs for Wilcoxson, but he had demurred, insisting that they'd better stick to their schedule, otherwise they risked losing Lennon.

Whatever.

"Let us get down to it," Wilcoxson said from a master control booth equipped with a video monitor overlooking both the lounge and studio. *"You committed a particular crime yesterday, one that resulted in the exchange of $650,000. To spare your girlfriend, you will bring that money here, and give it to Mr. Fieuchevsky."*

Wilcoxson watched Lennon's face on the monitor carefully. He didn't react, but he knew that inside, the guy had to be reeling. Wilcoxson badly wanted to make him flinch. Just once. Make him speak. Plead. Beg.

Instead, Lennon just gave them the finger.

Wilcoxson exhaled, then started speaking again. *"Mr. Lennon, you don't know—*

Cigar
Time

—ABOUT YOUR GIRLFRIEND'S CONDITION, DO YOU?"
Condition. Hmmm.
"We've left you something on the couch. Go ahead. Take a look."
Lennon lowered his left pistol slightly, then looked. There was a
white plastic wand resting on top of a pillow. Careful to keep his
right hand aimed at the Russian—useless gesture as it was—
Lennon tucked his other pistol in his waistband and slowly walked
to the couch. He picked up the object. It looked like a thermome-
ter case, with a little plastic window. The space inside the window
was white, except for a thin blue line that bisected it.
*"It's not easy, getting a urine sample from an unwilling woman.
We had to bring her around again, force her to submit, then render
her unconscious for our own safety. Chloroform is a nasty, sloppy
chemical. Crude."*
Lennon stared at the blue line, finally realizing.
"Not good for the baby."
Realizing how stupid he had been.
That explained the secrecy, the weird moods. Of course. She
hadn't wanted to distract him from the bank plans. That was Katie.
Anything important always waited until after a job. More connec-
tions formed in Lennon's head. That was why she had insisted on
somewhere nice—a resort—even though they had spent most of
the winter lazing around. She had wanted the day to be special. An
infusion of cash, a beautiful view, sunshine, an announcement.
Pregnant.
But who . . . ?
Lennon felt the room tip slightly on its axis.

Three
For
Flinching

WILCOXSON SAW IT: LENNON'S FACE TWITCHED. HIS knees even appeared to buckle for an instant. He had gotten to him. Hit him in the space between the plates of armor. Lennon was going to do anything he wanted. The rest was academic.

"*So listen carefully, Mr. Lennon. Listen to mommy.*"

Wilcoxson pressed PLAY, and the tape he'd prepared started spinning.

"*Patrick, it's me. The time is 11:43, Saturday, March 30th. I am here in Philadelphia, not elsewhere as previously arranged. I came back. They tell me you're alive, and that you are supposed to bring them what they want, otherwise they're going to kill me. This is what they told me to say. I'll be unharmed and released if you do what they say.*" A pause; some murmuring. "*See you soon.*"

Wilcoxson pressed STOP, then looked at Lennon on the video screen. The poor guy was working hard, trying to keep the emotions about Katie stuffed out of the way. After all, Wilcoxson had taught him years ago that the secret to any successful heist was taking human failure out of the equation. That meant taking humanity out of the equation. Hunger, lust, anger, joy had no place in a bank robbery. Somebody pops your partner, the guy you've been pulling heists with since fifth grade? Forget about it. Cry later; make your getaway now.

But this was easier said than done. Wilcoxson was sure that Lennon could think of nothing but Katie, and what might be happening to her. Russian fuckers, doping her and forcing her to pee into a cup. Rough hands over her. Tying her up. Stripping her.

Probably smirking. Yes, Wilcoxson was sure it was eating Lennon up alive. It would eat him up, too, if the roles were reversed.

"I want you to drop those guns."

And Lennon instantly lowered them. The man had a strange, blank look on his face, as if the only way to keep emotion in check was to completely unplug from reality.

"Drop them. On the ground."

He did, like a zombie.

"Good. You're on your way to saving the lives of your girlfriend and your unborn child. And by the way, congratulations. Now Mr. Fieuchevsky has a few parting words for you, before you go to recover the money."

The Russian needed no prodding. He emerged from the booth, shotgun in hand, with a wicked smile like a Doberman bearing its teeth.

Wilcoxson had to watch this very carefully. Fieuchevsky had insisted on something, *anything,* to calm the raging forces inside. They had spent fifteen minutes up in Wilcoxson's Rittenhouse Square apartment negotiating how much punishment Lennon should receive this afternoon. The Russian wanted carte blanche; as long as the bank robber could walk, he could recover the money. Wilcoxson said no, absolutely not. You can't demoralize him right away. You have to give him some shred of hope, get what you want, then crush him like a bug. Save some for later, Evsei, he'd pleaded. You'll get your chance.

The negotiations got down to specifics: after a heated exchange, Wilcoxson finally agreed to allow the Russian three body blows with the butt of the shotgun. No head, no chest, no groin. Then let Lennon walk away, and go bring back the money.

Personally, Wilcoxson thought the internal pain—wondering what was happening to Katie this afternoon—was punishment enough. But the Russian thought differently.

And as it turned out, Fieuchevsky threw all their negotiations out the window. The first blow was a rifle-butt hit to the face.

Lennon's head snapped in the opposite direction, and a geyser of crimson fluid sprayed out of his mouth. He staggered backward, hands flailing out, reaching for something to steady himself. Christ, this Russian was a cocksucker.

Second blow: right to the chest, while Lennon was recovering from the first. A jackhammer shot to the ribs and protective sack around the heart. Jesus. Lennon was powerless to fight back. Fighting back would mean disaster for Katie.

Wilcoxson could have announced the third blow ahead of time. Of course. Groin. Now Lennon was on the floor, clawing at the industrial carpet, presumably trying to dig his way out of the studio. The man had better pray Katie carried this baby to term; it didn't look like Lennon was going to have much luck reproducing in the future. Not with a shot like that.

Wilcoxson had to intervene when it looked like Fieuchevsky was going for a fourth, a fifth, and maybe even a seventeenth shot. He pressed the mike button and said: *"Go now, Mr. Lennon. Save your family's life. Report here tomorrow. Noon."*

Fieuchevsky stood there, rifle hoisted up in the air with both hands, looking confused. Then he remembered himself and lowered the gun. He looked as disappointed as a man could.

Lennon crawled out of the studio.

Wilcoxson flicked off the mike and breathed. This might actually work.

"Shit," said Holden Richards, standing up from behind the partition. "Remind me never to be on the other side of that gun."

anatomy
of
a
Double
Cross

HOLDEN HAD BEEN HIDING BEHIND THAT FUCKING partition for an hour now, waiting for Lennon to show up. It wasn't comfortable, and his neck and back ached like a mother-fucker after that crazy shit yesterday.

Yesterday.

Fifteen minutes after the Wachovia job.

Wilcoxson had said, No sweat. The Russians are gonna pull their van out in front of you guys, surround you, put hoods over your heads, take you somewhere, pop the other guys, let you go.

Yeah, they pulled their van out all right.

Best Holden could figure it, Lennon was going too fast, and the Russians didn't have time to get out in front like they had planned. So they just gunned it, and smashed right into the Subaru.

Sure, Holden had been bracing for a sudden stop, but not *that* fucking kind of stop. The Forester achieved liftoff, spun in the air a couple of times, landed top-first on the wet mud next to the Schuylkill River, then slid a while, so long that Holden was start-ing to think they were going to end up in the river, and that would be it. But no. The car skidded to a halt, the Russians got their act together and finally—finally—surrounded them with those crazy black submachine guns they got, but it didn't matter. Lennon was gone, convulsing and spitting before he passed out. Bling was still awake, so Holden started hammering his face with his elbow. Who cares? Nigger was going down a tube anyway.

Truth be told, Holden felt a little bad about Bling. He was the guy who'd introduced him to Wilcoxson in the first place, vouched for him. Holden had no idea there was a loose network of dudes in his profession, scattered across the country. It was like the Mafia, but not, at the same time. Just guys who knew other guys, vouching for each other. So Bling vouched for Holden, and met Wilcoxson one night for dinner at that steak joint, Smith and Wollensky, had himself a fat Montana prime rib. Wilcoxson told him he had a future. He could always spot talent, he said.

And that was it. Then nothing, for months. Bling used him for a couple of jobs, nothing big. Wilcoxson didn't call him for shit.

Which bugged Holden.

Bling was fine, but he never tapped him for the big heists, the kind that Wilcoxson said he was ready to pull. He wanted Wilcoxson to give him something that would set him up. He was tired of kicking around his same old West Philly apartment. You didn't see Bling around the neighborhood—Negro was out kickin' it in resort hotels.

So when the call finally came from Wilcoxson a few weeks back, Holden said yes, not even a thought to it.

The call from Bling came the next day. Wilcoxson had vouched for *him,* instead of Bling doin' it the other way around. A nice fat score, Bling told him. "Don't fuck it up," he said. Yeah, yeah, yeah. Keep flapping your gums there, Bling. Holden knew what Wilcoxson was *really* up to, and Bling didn't. Fuck Bling. This was his ticket in. No more West Philly decaying mansion shit—hello, resort hotel circuit.

Wilcoxson told him, "Holden, I need somebody I can trust." The implication: Bling was somebody he couldn't trust. All Holden had to do, Wilcoxson said, was keep him posted, and then have a little patience right after the job.

A little patience, yeah. And a motherfucking neck brace.

After the Russians took Bling and Lennon away—they stripped them naked and put their corpses in body bags and everything—Holden wanted to go right after the money. His gut told him to grab it and run. Forget Wilcoxson, who had promised half of the proceeds instead of the third Bling had promised. Half, third. Why not take it all?

No. That wasn't thinking big picture. Wilcoxson could set him up. $650,000 was nothing compared to what was in the future.

Cops watch parking lots right after, Wilcoxson explained. You don't want to go anywhere near that car. It'll be there. Don't worry. Holden couldn't help worrying. Is this how the pros really did it? Bling and Lennon didn't seem worried. Wilcoxson didn't seem worried. But it bugged the living shit out of Holden, leaving that kind of money behind, just sitting in a parking lot in the middle of the city.

Holden spent the rest of Friday laying low, trying to keep his mind off the car and the money. Watched a few DVDs, had some take-out sushi and some Ketel One vodka, in honor of the Russians, who were down by the river that night putting Bling and Lennon down the tube. Holden looked around his cluttered apartment—the one they had used to plan the heist—and thought about packing up his shit. Actually packed up some shit, then stopped to have some more Ketel One.

Saturday morning, hungover, he got the call from Wilcoxson. There were some "complications."

Lennon was still alive.

"Go get the car," Wilcoxson said. "Then call me back."

The car meaning the money. Holden had a really bad feeling about this. They couldn't have listened to him yesterday? Listened to how motherfucking stupid it was to leave that much money just sittin' around in a parking lot?

Holden hopped a SEPTA green-line trolley out to Nineteenth and Market, then walked the few blocks to the lot. He walked up and down the rows, looking. He looked some more, then went back over everything again.

No car.

No car, no money.

He called Wilcoxson, who was in the middle of some weird shit, it sounded like, and told him the bad news.

"Fucking Lennon," he said. "Okay, hang tight. I'm going to call you back."

Twenty minutes went by before Wilcoxson called him back. "I want you to meet me at my apartment. We're going to get our money back. Bring somebody you can trust."

Sounded good to Holden. He just hadn't counted on crouching down behind a sound partition for close to an hour waiting for that mute bastard.

Finally, Lennon arrived and there was some back and forth, with Wilcoxson talking to him over a speaker, his voice all modified and shit. Holden was impressed; Wilcoxson had pulled together a plan fairly quickly, even with the Russian involved. "Don't worry about the Russian being there," Wilcoxson had told Holden over the phone. "We're going to take care of him today. Let him join his son."

And now, there Lennon went, broken and gushing, out the door again, off to recover the $650,000 from wherever he'd stashed it. If he wanted to see his knocked-up ho again, he would be bringing it back here tomorrow, high noon.

Holden stood up from his hiding spot and his knees cracked. Shit. He was stiff as hell, and his neck and back still hurt from that car wreck yesterday.

He felt the pistol in the right pocket of his starter jacket. The plan was, wait for the Russian to come out of the booth, along with Wilcoxson. Then, when Wilcoxson gave the signal, he was supposed to shoot the Russian in the head. "The studio is soundproof—nobody's going to hear a thing," Wilcoxson had reassured him.

Here came the Russian, holding his own gun in his hands. The

Russian smiled uncomfortably at Holden. Holden nodded back, careful to show no expression on his face.

"That went fairly well, didn't it?" said Wilcoxson, who popped out of a small door to the right. "Tomorrow, Evsei, you will have your revenge, and some money to ease the pain."

The Russian nodded. He didn't look happy about the arrangements. Not at all. He certainly wasn't going to be happy about what Wilcoxson had planned, either.

Then again, neither was Holden.

Why settle for $325,000? He already knew the whole deal. Lennon was bringing the cash from the Wachovia job here tomorrow, in exchange for his woman.

Holden shot the Russian in the head first.

Wilcoxson looked surprised—he hadn't given the signal yet. But not half as surprised as when Holden pointed the gun at *him*.

There was nothing to worry about. The studio was soundproof.

SATURDAY P.M. [LATER]

I can imagine them hitting the sack after one of those robberies, just laughing their heads off and having fun.

— PSYCHOLOGIST FRANK FARLEY, ON
BANK ROBBERS CRAIG PRITCHERT
AND NOVA GUTHRIE

The House on Oregon Avenue

ALL THINGS CONSIDERED, IT WAS QUITE A BARGAIN: An empty row house in South Philly.

A doctor, with malpractice insurance problems and a suspended license, to attend to his multiple wounds.

Bottle of Jameson. Stack of frozen dinners and a small microwave.

Bottle of aspirin.

Plastic digital alarm clock.

Two pistols—both .38 Sig Sauers.

Six boxes of ammunition.

Price tag: $325,000.

Lennon had returned to Dominick's restaurant that afternoon and put forth a straightforward business proposition, in writing: He needed food, shelter, and medical attention. In return, Perelli would receive $325,000, half of the proceeds from the Wachovia job, upon its recovery. He wrote that the Russians had his girlfriend, and that they demanded the money from the Wachovia heist or they were going to execute her. And their unborn child. Perelli was a father; Lennon didn't think it would hurt to play on the man's familial sympathies. He added that he had a plan to recover the bank loot, as well as bury the Russians. All he needed was time to recover and heal.

And think about his familial sympathies later.

Perelli agreed.

Perelli not only agreed, but had insisted on the suit, too. He got off on the whole idea of Lennon as a heister under his employ.

"A bank robber can't be running around in a Father fuckin' Judge sweatshirt, for fuck's sake," he'd said. "Did Machine Gun Kelly wear a sweatshirt? Did Johnny Dillinger?"

So when Perelli dispatched the unlicensed sawbones, he also sent along a guy to take Lennon's measurements. The suit would be ready in a couple of hours, Perelli promised.

Lennon didn't really care about the suit. He cared about getting Katie back, getting the money back, and getting the fuck out of Philadelphia. Then he would think about this baby thing. It was too much right now. In the meantime, he ate, he drank enough to dull the pain, he rested. He woke up when the doctor arrived, and tried not to cry out when the doc mauled sensitive parts. Listened to him *tsk-tsk,* then resume work. Cautioned Lennon against drinking. Whatever. Then the doctor scribbled his pager number on a blue napkin and left. Lennon drank more Jameson's and fell back asleep.

The doorbell rang. It was a young kid, delivering the suit. A black Ermenegildo Zegna, from a shop called Boyd's on Chestnut Street. Included was a dark blue Stacy Adams dress shirt, black socks with dark blue clocks on them, and a pair of black Giorgio Brutini shoes with a single strap buckle. Perelli had also thrown in a pair of sunglasses—Dior Homme by Hedi Slimane. The only items not plucked directly from the pages of British GQ were some undergarments by Hanes. Jesus fuck, tighty-whiteys. They must have been a personal favorite of Perelli's.

Lennon took a slow, wince-inducing shower. His face was tragic-looking; in places, it had the pattern of a tie-dyed shirt in blacks and purples and blues. But he was pleasantly surprised to find that all of the clothes fit perfectly. Even the tighty-whiteys. He dressed himself, even putting on the Giorgio Brutinis. He loaded the Sig Sauers, then put one in each jacket pocket. He pressed two fingers against his carotid artery.

Then he lay down on top of the single mattress sitting in the middle of the empty master bedroom, and closed his eyes.

A few fevered hours later, his eyes popped open.

Three seconds later, the alarm went off. He was already dressed.

It was time to go.

The Grave By the River

HOLDEN RICHARDS FOUND THE PIPE, NO SWEAT. Mikal, the Russian's kid, had told him about it. Over on the Camden side, not too far from the bridge. That narrowed it down. There wasn't too much new construction over here near the bridge—with the aquarium, and the Tweeter Center, and the rest of the tourist crap—tourists in Camden, if you can believe it— hardly enough room for a cockroach with a hard-on to squeeze through.

But here they were, trying to fit another tourist attraction along the cramped waterfront. A children's museum.

Boy, would the kids be surprised to discover what Uncle Holden was dumping down their drainage pipe.

First down, the Russian. Let him and his kid have a happy reunion together. The Russian's head remained remarkably intact, despite the point-blank shot to his face. The bullet entered his forehead, then exploded on its way out of the skull. The back of his head was shit, but his sturdy good looks would be preserved for the ages. As he let go of the Russian's ankles, Holden wondered if he and his boy would end up cheek to cheek in the pipe, and what future archeologists would make of that.

Next up: Wilcoxson. Bank robber extraordinaire. His face hadn't fared as well. Holden had popped a cap straight on, and Wilcoxson's face was pretty much ripped off, leaving a mess of pulp behind. He screamed for a while, his legs flailing around like he was riding an invisible bicycle. Thank God for the soundproofing, huh? Eventually, the fury died, and so did Wilcoxson.

At the time, Holden had been tempted to go back and pop a cap in the bitch, too, just to get it over with. Lennon would show up tomorrow with the $650,000 no matter what, and then Holden would kill him. Right now, she was stashed at Wilcoxson's Rittenhouse Square pad, with his cousin Derek keeping an eye on her. Wilcoxson had agreed to that plan, but he'd also seemed nervous about letting some other dude hang with her while she was handcuffed to a pole. Like he was her man, or something. Something hinky was up there.

Holden thought about it for a while, then realized there really was no good reason to keep her alive. He picked up his cell and dialed Derek.

Bathroom with a Book

LISA PERELLI KEYED INTO THE FRONT DOOR, AND IMMEdiately felt this weird vibe. Somebody else was here. Had her father rented this place out without telling her?

Of course, why would he tell her?

She was here to pick up Andrew's things. This house on Oregon Avenue was one of many that her father owned. It was the one she had used during the past six weeks. Her and Andrew.

Lisa hated Andrew's dorm room—it was like a shoebox, only with worse interior design. Andrew, meanwhile, hated camping out on the couch at Lisa's father's place in South Philly. Andrew never said why until one day, a month and a half ago, when he finally broke down and admitted the truth: he couldn't use the bathroom at her father's house. Not the way he usually did in the mornings. Andrew veiled it in all kinds of cute terms—I'm a regular guy, I need to read in the morning—but Lisa knew what he was talking about. Funny thing was, Lisa was the same way. That's why she hated crashing at the dorms. She just couldn't feel comfortable getting up, walking down a hallway past a bunch of strange doors with strange boys behind them, walking up two flights of stairs, then using the common women's bathroom. She wasn't used to that sort of thing. That's why she never chose to live on campus in the first place.

The only solution: Dad's Oregon Avenue rental property, complete with one and a half baths. A full bathroom upstairs, and another smaller one on the first floor.

It was like playing house, only without the risk. Andrew had some minor things there—an Aerobed, a stack of paperback books, extra contact lenses, and a cardboard box with underwear, deodorant, a toothbrush, and a huge tube of Crest. Lisa brought candles and stored jug bottles of Pinot Grigio in the fridge, and stacked some of her unmentionables neatly in the master bedroom closet.

Her dad didn't know they stayed there; Lisa had filched the keys one night.

The same keys that were in her hand now, still halfway jammed into the front-door lock.

Lisa listened.

Somebody was definitely here. Upstairs.

She closed the door behind her and locked it.

Gamma

Delta

Gazelle

I T WASN'T THAT KATIE ESPECIALLY MINDED BEING HAND-cuffed to a pole all day. She could deal with that. She didn't even mind the tender bruising on her face from where that Russian had punched her. She could deal with that, too.

What she couldn't deal with: how badly she needed to pee.

It was a pregnancy thing.

Katie was in Henry's bedroom, that much she knew. She'd been in here once before, when he'd given her and Patrick the grand tour. She didn't expect her next visit to Henry's bedroom to involve loss of consciousness, handcuffs, and a support column, around which her arms were secured backward, behind her back. Henry didn't seem like the kinky type.

After the Russian had decked her, she'd woken up on the couch. The Russian had a black revolver pressed to the back of Henry's head. "They want you to make a tape recording," he said calmly, his eyes trying to communicate something else. "I suggest we do what they say, then sort this out later."

Katie didn't argue the point. She had felt bad—she obviously had led the Russian right here and gotten Henry tangled up in this. Patrick would have never involved Henry. Not for a million bucks. She was disgusted with herself. There was so much she needed to learn.

Michael kept telling her that. Not in a snide way. Just in his typical, nonjudgmental, matter-of-fact way. Michael was a real professional. It's what had attracted her to him in the first place.

Katie spoke the words Henry gave her into the tape recorder, trying to reassure Patrick by how calm she could sound. As if nothing were wrong. She tried to think of a code word, something to let Patrick know where she was, but couldn't think of anything. It all happened too fast.

There was a knock at the door. The Russian forced Henry up to answer it. It was two young-looking white boys who desperately wanted to look black. They didn't look at Henry. She didn't know them, but she started putting the pieces together. One of the white boys was probably the third guy on the Wachovia job—aside from Lennon and Bling. And this third guy had sold the job out to the Russians.

The thicker of the two white boys handcuffed her to a support column in Henry's bedroom. Henry tried to reassure her: "Everything's going to be fine"—before he was hustled out the door with the other white boy and the Russian. They were off to find Patrick. Or threaten him. Or kill him. Or bring him back here, then threaten and kill him. That was probably it. Why else would the Russian keep her alive?

Fifteen minutes later, it first occurred to Katie that she had to pee.

Thirty minutes later, she knew she was going to have to do something drastic, or otherwise wet herself. As well as Henry's fancy Pergo bedroom floor.

"Hey."

Her captor. He was a young-looking blond-haired Alpha Chi thick-neck, complete with college sweatshirt and scuffed baggy pants. Joe Frat, with a heavy pistol. He obviously wasn't a member of the Russian *mafiya;* he was an errand boy. An extremely odd choice for an errand boy.

"Want a blow job?"

It took some more sweet talk, but the Alpha Chi thick-neck eventually agreed to her proposal. After all, he'd led a life where it was easy to believe that random women wanted nothing more than to take his cock into their mouths. But he was no fool, this boy. First, he made her promise that she wouldn't use any teeth. Katie promised. Then she asked him if he wouldn't mind servicing her first, otherwise, it would just be demeaning. Alpha Chi eagerly agreed to her amendment to the proposal. That sounded even better—she must be really into him. The thick-neck said he really liked doing that. He probably had a very satisfied Gamma Delta gazelle somewhere in the city.

He dropped to his knees, then unbuttoned Katie's jeans and lowered the zipper.

"Be gentle with me," she cooed, and waited for him to look up at her.

When he did, she smashed her knee into his Adam's apple. It was the most effective way to kill a man with a single body part, be it the flat of a hand, an elbow, or a knee. Patrick had taught her that. Joe Frat died fairly quickly, scraping the Pergo floors with his thick monkey-boy fingers until they stopped twitching.

The only problem was: she had no way of searching him for a key.

She had no way to contact Michael.

And she still very badly, very desperately, had to pee.

Many, many hours later, the cell phone in the corpse's pants pocket rang.

No

One

Answers

LENNON STOLE A CAR A FEW BLOCKS AWAY FROM THE safe house in South Philly, then drove up Twentieth Street all the way to Center City. The clouds were low and the wind was cold. Lennon found a parking spot on Rittenhouse Square, miraculously enough. The doorman didn't bother with him, once he told him where he was headed. Lennon put his ear to Wilcoxson's door and listened, then knocked.

Fuck.

There was no answer.

Wilcoxson was his ace in the hole—the only guy in Philadelphia he could trust. Lennon hadn't clued him in to the Wachovia heist ahead of time; better for Wilcoxson not to know. The old man had retired from the business years ago. No sense dragging him into something that could come back to bite him on the arse. Still, Wilcoxson had always been there for him in the past, and there was no reason not to go to him now. Lennon felt hopelessly outnumbered—Russian and Italian gangsters here, rogue cops there. This wasn't his city. He needed help, protection. A few hours just to breathe. Wilcoxson could give that to him. Mentor to mentee, one last time. For old time's sake.

But Wilcoxson wasn't home.

Double fuck.

Lennon walked back down the hallway to the elevator, then took a car down to the lobby again. He scanned the lobby, hoping he might see Wilcoxson, lazing about, maybe kissing a Rittenhouse Square socialite good night, until we meet again, blah blah blah. Lennon had always wanted money just to live. Wilcoxson wanted money to buy a better life. The old man had grown up dirt poor in Brooklyn and clawed his way up and out during the 1960s. He never wanted to go back.

Lennon knew he couldn't stay in this lobby forever. He was wearing a sharp Italian suit, but he still looked like he had gone six rounds with a piece of industrial machinery. And lost. The Rittenhouse Hotel management would get nervous soon.

Triple fuck.

This is the way it always was. Lennon hated asking for help. He absolutely *loathed* it. Lennon grew up promising himself he would never ask his father for anything as long as he lived—his father considered basic food and run-down shelter in a bad neighborhood gifts enough—and Lennon stuck to that promise. Even in jail. Self-reliance was always his preferred course.

But the moment he broke down and decided that asking for help was the most reasonable course, help was suddenly not available. There was no one to turn to. There was no help in this world. You were always lugging the load by yourself. Surround yourself with family, with loved ones, with minions, with partners, with whoever. But the truth remained: everyone has to do it alone.

Lennon exited the hotel lobby and started walking toward Locust Street. He was so absorbed in his own thoughts, he almost didn't see him.

The dead man, walking out of the park.

Kick

Back

FUCKING DEREK. HE NEVER TURNED HIS CELL PHONE on. What was the point of owning one of the fucking things if you never turned it on? So instead of chilling out for a couple of hours like he had promised himself—hey, throwing dead bodies down a fucking pipe is still hard work, no matter how you cut it—he was forced to drive all the way back down to Center City to check in on Derek and Lennon's bitch.

The doorman looked at him funny at first, then regained his composure. He must have remembered him from this morning, when Wilcoxson had called for him. That was the way it was going to be from now on. Instant respect. Especially with that $650 large all to himself. Maybe he'd buy Wilcoxson's apartment with some of the money. The old guy sure wasn't going to be needing it anymore.

Holden took the elevator up. He keyed into Wilcoxson's apartment and called out. "Yo, Derr."

Nothing.

He walked into the bedroom and saw his cousin on the floor, dead. The girl was still handcuffed to the pole, but it looked like she was dead, too. Water was all over the floor, like someone had dumped a wash bucket. What the fuck?

Holden kneeled over Derek and felt his neck for a pulse. Not that he'd really know what to check for, but his skin was cold anyway, so there wasn't any need to get scientific about it. Derek's neck felt funny—aside from being cold.

Holden turned back around, and just in time.

The bitch was yelling and throwing a knee at his face.

I.

O.

You

EFORE JOHNNY KOTKIEWICZ TOOK A JOB AS HEAD OF security for the Rittenhouse Towers, he worked as a Philly cop, and eventually ended up in the Robbery/Homicide Division. He put in his twenty, then retired to the private sector. The Rittenhouse made him a nice offer; he accepted it. The money came in handy for his daughter, who was attending Villanova Law School. Maybe someday she would work for one of those high-toned Center City firms—Schnaeder Harrison, Soliss-Cohen—and afford to buy into this condominium, instead of working the entrance like her old man.

He was proud of what he did. But he wanted better for his daughter. Same old parenting story.

Kotkiewicz was here late on a Saturday night, which was un-usual. But this had been an unusual day at the Rittenhouse. A cast of unusual characters had been floating around all day. First, a pretty young redhead, around 7 A.M. She went up to room 910, which belonged to Mr. Henry Wilcoxson, a Center City financial consultant. (At least, that's what it said in the Rittenhouse security files.) Not unusual in itself. But the redhead left twenty minutes later. Later that morning, a beefy man who looked Slavic—Bosnian, Russian, maybe—also went up to room 910. An hour later, the redhead returned and took the elevator straight up to room 910. Barely twenty minutes later, a guy who looked like that white rapper—Eminem—entered the lobby, along with a doughier white guy. Their destination? Yep, 910. Forty minutes later, Mr. Wilcoxson, the Slavic gentleman, and Eminem left the building together. The doughy guy and the redhead were still upstairs.

It was an odd assortment of people and behaviors, and odd collections made Kotkiewicz nervous. He was familiar with the daily patterns of Rittenhouse residents, as well as their guests, but this was something he'd never seen before.

He made a phone call or two, and had a few things faxed over to him. Following a hunch. Like always.

So Kotkiewicz decided to stick around. Judy wasn't thrilled; she was looking forward to Johnny bringing home some takeout from Kum-Lin's and she had rented a movie, *Road to Perdition*. This was the same old story, too; Kotkiewicz torn between the work, and the wife.

As the evening wore on, Kotkiewicz thought maybe he'd been foolish.

And then another stranger entered the lobby and made a beeline for room 910. Mr. Wilcoxson's pad again. He was obviously joining the redhead and the doughy boy. But for what?

Five minutes later, the new stranger—a brown-haired, blue-eyed guy with the nastiest set of facial bruises he'd ever seen—stepped off the elevator and walked out of the lobby.

Barely a minute passed. And then:

Eminem walked into the lobby again. Kotkiewicz was prepared. Eminem nodded at him, then Kotkiewicz threw a last look at the I.O. sitting on his desk. He'd been studying it all afternoon, trying to rely on his memory. But this last glance clinched it. *Bingo.* Holden Richards. Suspect in the Wachovia bank heist the day before.

Then he flipped to another I.O. Richards was one of three guys.

Hot damn. The other stranger. Mr. Purple Bruises.

Kotkiewicz picked up the phone. When he looked up, Bruises was walking back into the lobby.

Surgical
Grade

IBET YOU THINK I'M PISSED OFF 'BOUT MY COUSIN HERE."
She didn't reply.

"Well, you know, I'm not. Not really."

Nothing.

"I'm all bidness tonight. You know what I'm saying?"

Nothing.

"Alright, play it hard. I can play it hard, too." The white guy—
the other white guy from this morning, this was—stood up. "Be
right back."

Katie watched him walk out of the bedroom. She looked
around the room one last time—was there something she had
missed? Something that would get her out of these handcuffs?
No, of course there wouldn't be. She'd been looking all afternoon,
all evening, all night. The digital clock on Henry's dresser was out
of view. She could see the imitation wood-grain top, but not the
numbers. She had no idea what time it was. And she had no idea
how she was going to get out of this one.

Her entire body ached; her shoulder muscles were starting to
spasm. She had lost control of her bladder more times than she
cared to remember.

The white guy walked back into the bedroom. He was holding
a kitchen knife.

Wonderful.

What would Michael say, if he could see her now?

"I know you're knocked up and all. Wilcoxson told me all about
it. And I was there when he told your old man. Boy, did he look
surprised."

Katie didn't look at him, but her mind was reeling. If this little idiot was telling the truth, it was a cruel disappointment. The news was supposed to have been delivered in the warm breeze, with cold flutes of champagne in hand. Not here in Philadelphia. Not by Henry.

Why did Henry tell Patrick about the baby? Jesus, was he trying to make the Russian feel *sorry* for all of them? Playing the unborn-baby card?

She could only imagine what Patrick must be thinking.

"You want me to do you a favor?" the white boy asked, kneeling closer to her, holding the tip of the knife up to her nose. "How about I give you an abortion, solve all your problems?"

Katie looked at the knife handle. It was a Tenmijuraku, one of those high-end Japanese kitchen knives made with a single piece of surgical stainless steel. Henry enjoyed cooking, and insisted on owning the best kitchen tools. The white boy wielding the knife, however, probably didn't appreciate the difference. Tenmijuraku, Ginsu, whatever. As long as it could slice a tin can in half. Or a woman, handcuffed to a pole in a luxury apartment.

This white boy comes anywhere near my legs with that thing, Katie thought, I'm going to pummel him with my knees. Or try to.

Unfortunately, that's exactly what seemed to be on the white boy's mind.

Ta Tuirse Orm

LENNON TRIED THE DOORKNOB; AS HE SUSPECTED, IT was open. Henry. Holden. The failed heist. Too many coincidences; he'd sort them out later. He took one of the Sig Sauers out of his jacket pocket—he'd stashed the other one downstairs, in the park—and slowly edged his way into Wilcoxson's apartment. No sign of anybody in the living room. He heard a voice speaking in the bedroom, which was down a short hallway. He edged around corners, taking it nice and cautious. But the only people in the apartment, it seemed, were in the bedroom.

A dead guy, facedown on the floor. The back of what appeared to be Holden Richards's head. And Katie, handcuffed backward to a pole.

Holden was holding a butcher knife in one hand and trying to loosen Katie's pants with his other hand. The button on her jeans was already undone, the gold zipper halfway down.

Relief flooded Lennon. Katie was alive. Even better, she was alive, and not guarded by a phalanx of beefy Russian gangsters. Just Holden, the little fuck.

Soon to be *ex*-fuck.

Katie saw him and smirked. She was still here.

"My *brother's* back, and you're *gonna* be in trouble," she sang softly.

Holden's head whipped around, knife in hand, fabric in the other, looking like the cover of a rape counseling video. His mouth flopped open.

"Lennon? Who told you to come here?"

Lennon responded by aiming the gun at his face.

"The only reason he's not shooting," said Katie, "is that he doesn't want to get blood all over me. Now put the knife on the floor, fuck-o, and crawl backward."

Holden seemed to think this over; the knife in his hand jumped a bit. But after realizing that his only option—stabbing the girl, getting shot in the head—wasn't a good one, he relented. The knife clanged when it hit the floor.

"Now kiss the floor, facedown. That's it. Slide away . . . slowly. Toward the bed. Uh-huh. By the way, you know that wet stuff you're lying in? It's piss. Never handcuff a pregnant woman to a pole all day."

Lennon watched Holden shudder.

"The keys to these cuffs are in the dead guy's pocket," Katie said. "I hope."

Lennon checked both front pockets; the keys were in the left. He uncuffed Katie, then gently helped her crawl to a lying position on a dry spot of the floor. Katie touched his cheek, ran a thumb across his chin. She smirked again. Lennon winked. He leaned in close to her ear. He whispered: *"Cén chaoi a bhfuil tú?"*

"Ta tuirse orm," she replied.

Lennon was supposed to be a mute. But too many people could interpret sign language. So Lennon had taught Katie—who had been born in Massachusetts, not Ireland—some Gaelic, which they used in secret, or in sign. She told him she was tired.

Lennon walked over to Holden. His objective was now relatively simple: Holden had sold the Wachovia job to somebody. Lennon needed to know who, and where the money was now. He wasn't very good at the heavy stuff—even in bank situations—but the way things were going, Lennon didn't think he'd have too much trouble improvising on the spot.

Something caught his eye. An iridescent flash of blue reflecting from a window in Wilcoxson's bedroom.

"Patrick," Katie said.

She'd seen it, too.

Blue, then red lights, flickering through the air outside the window.

Repenthouse

LENNON ONCE READ AN ENCYCLOPEDIA THAT LISTED everyone who was ever on the FBI's Ten Most Wanted list. Many Top Tenners, as the FBI called them, were bank robbers, and Lennon skipped to those first. It was interesting. Whenever a bank robber made the top ten, it usually fit a particular pattern: three or four guys hit a series of banks, then in the last job, some cop or citizen gets killed. Three guys scatter, and two of them inevitably get picked up within thirty-six hours. The third guy usually goes the distance.

The lesson: if you can manage to make it past the first thirty-six hours, you have a strong chance of going the distance, making a long run. Of course, your captured compadres might rat you out, so it's best to avoid your usual haunts, especially the place where you planned the caper.

It was rapidly approaching the thirty-six-hour mark, and there were two heisters still at large. Lennon and Holden. The cops were outside.

Lennon decided he wasn't going to be the one picked up. He was going for the big run.

They had no idea how many were waiting outside, or if the Feds were involved. They had no escape routes in mind; neither of them knew the building all that well.

"And what do we do with him?" Katie asked, gesturing to the bedroom door. Lennon had gagged Holden, then handcuffed him, face-forward, to the pole. Then he'd locked him in there with his dead friend.

Killing Holden would be a waste. Lennon was already responsible for the deaths of at least six people, and that was about six over his personal limit. He used to pride himself on his choice of a nonviolent criminal profession.

"Let the FBI have at him," Lennon whispered.

"Does he know anything about Wachovia?"

"Nothing important."

"Okay then."

There wasn't much time left. If the guy down at the desk had any brains, he'd know the exact door through which to send the police.

"Let me grab my luggage, and let's go," Katie said. "That's a nice suit, by the way. It almost distracts from your face."

"Tell you about it later," Lennon said, still taking care to keep his voice low. He didn't know if Holden could hear them or not, and he still wanted to keep his speaking voice a secret.

Up or down? Katie decided they should go up. The Feds would expect their fugitives to see flashing lights and try to scramble for the exits. That's why they flashed the lights in the first place. There were eleven more floors above Wilcoxson's apartment. Plenty of places to hide. If they could find a cooperative neighbor.

"Do we have a plan?" Lennon asked.

"Yes," Katie said. "We knock. If nobody answers, we go in. If somebody answers, we show them that gun of yours—nice gun, by the way."

"Tell you about it later."

"Did it come with the suit?"

Lennon smirked at her.

They settled on the eighteenth floor. Not quite the luxe penthouses, but nice enough views to guarantee some serious space. Better to keep someone under wraps in a bigger place. You could isolate them in one room, move around in the others. Breathe a little, plan your next move.

"Which one?"

"That one. 1809. It's going to be my wedding date."

Lennon cocked his eyebrow. "Your what?"

"I'll tell you about it later. Ready?"

Katie knocked while Lennon pressed himself up against the outside wall, Sig Sauer clutched in both hands. Nothing. Katie glanced at Lennon and cocked her eyebrow. Lennon raised his index finger. Steady on.

Still nothing.

Lennon nodded. He handed the gun to Katie, who aimed it, chest-level, at the door. Katie stepped back and Lennon prepared to boot the bastard in.

A lock tumbled, then clicked into place. The door slowly opened.

Here we go.

Katie steeled herself. Waited for a face to appear. Lennon froze, mid-kick.

A guy in a tuxedo opened the door. But he didn't wait to see who was there. He turned around, without looking, and walked back down a long hallway. They could hear the faint din of conversation and a wailing saxophone, deep inside the penthouse. A party.

Katie shrugged, grabbed her luggage, and walked in.

There was a full bathroom just off the main hallway. Katie and Lennon went inside; Lennon locked the door behind them.

"You don't mind if I shower, do you?" Katie asked. "I had a series of accidents this afternoon and this evening."

Lennon turned his back to her and busied himself with her luggage.

"Want anything pressed, dearie?"

"Just hang the black Vera Wang on the back of the door. The steam will take care of the rest."

"Will do."

Katie took a brief shower. Brief for Katie meant ultra-brief; she never took more than five minutes anyway. It was Lennon who usually took his time under the hot spraying water. He always did his best thinking in his shower at home, among other personal hygiene locations.

She toweled off and looked at Lennon. "Where's the money?"

Lennon was secretly relieved. He didn't want to discuss the elephant in the room just yet. The eight-ounce elephant, tucked away in Katie's uterus. He was worried they would start discussing that, and who put it there, instead of how they were going to get their money and get out of there.

"I'll be fucked if I know," he said.

"The Russians don't have it, obviously. They wouldn't have bothered with me and that tape and everything else if they had. And it's fairly clear their coconspirator, your former partner, doesn't have it, either."

Lennon had been playing around with this in his head all night. Nix the Russians, and Holden. Who had the loot?

"Wilcoxson," he said.

"It's possible, but I don't think so. He's involved because I led the Russians here. Accidentally." She looked at him. "I might have been a bit careless this morning."

Lennon considered this, stared at Katie's belly. Nothing really showed yet. "I've been careless, too. I don't even want to tell you what the fuck I've been through."

"Your face certainly paints an interesting picture. As does the suit."

"Again with the suit?"

"It's awfully impressive," she said, drying her hair. "And here I thought you were lying dead in a ditch all this time."

"It was a pipe, but I'll save the wild stories for another night. We have three priorities: getting the fuck out of this building, getting our money, and getting the fuck out of this city."

"Don't you want to see the Liberty Bell?"

"Right. Almost forgot about that."

Forensics

L ISA WOKE UP AND STARED AT THE BLOODIED SWEAT-shirt again.

It had been balled up and pitched into a corner, along with a pair of wrinkled dress slacks, socks, and underwear. The underwear was definitely not Andrew's. When they'd first started dating, Andrew had worn tighty-whiteys—Fruit of the Loom. Gross! Old-man underwear. No matter how tough the guy, it made his legs look like little froggy legs poking out of a diaper.

Andrew loathed boxers; they were too baggy to wear under jeans, he said. So Lisa promptly escorted her American Express Gold card and Andrew to Boscov's, at the Franklin Mills Mall, where they settled on the next best thing: Fruit of the Loom boxer briefs. Lisa vetoed anything close to white; Andrew went home with a half-dozen three-packs of navy blue, black, and dark gray. The tighty-whiteys went into the weekly garbage.

The underwear balled up in the corner was a pair of blue-green plaid boxer shorts. Definitely not something Andrew would wear.

So whose were they?

The sweatshirt was a gray deal with navy blue letters: FATHER JUDGE HIGH SCHOOL emblazoned on the front. That wasn't Andrew's either—he was a St. Joe's Prep boy. Even more disturbing were the bloodstains, which were more black than red, and still wet to the touch (gross!), near the left shoulder. The sweatshirt reeked.

Lisa took another look at the dress slacks, at the label. Slates, size 34L, 30W. Andrew's size exactly. And Andrew's preferred label. He had two pair, which he wore Friday and Saturday nights alternately when he had gigs. Were these Andrew's pants?

And if so, why were they rolled up in a ball along with somebody else's clothes?

Off
Gardai

THE MOST INTERESTING PEOPLE AT THE PARTY WERE the drunk crime writer and the drunker chief of detectives. It was a writers' party. The host was new to Rittenhouse Towers, and new to money. Apparently he had written a surprise best-selling coffee-table book called *Barbers*. Page after page of black-and-white photographs of old South Philly barbers, posing with their customers, with tiny write-ups under each photograph telling each barber's life story in about 175 words.

For a reason known only to the American public, it was a runaway smash hit, spawning a calendar, date books, posters, an ABC television special, even a line of home hair-care tools. (Which seemed to negate the very job of the old-fashioned barber, but what the hell.) The forty-something writer sat back and watched the Brinks truck pull up and shovel bales of money into his living room. He traded in his dumpy Bella Vista one-bedroom for this five-bedroom spread in one of the city's most prestigious condos. Now he was preparing to compile a sort-of sequel, *Bartenders,* and had decided to show off to the rest of his old writer pals, many of whom were scraping by with $25,000-a-year gigs—if they were lucky—at one of the two competing weeklies.

All of this Lennon gathered in about twenty minutes of cocktail-conversation eavesdropping. The only thing flowing more freely than booze was the jealousy. The condo was absolutely lousy with it.

"You believe that? Six figures just for the calendar rights," said one guy in a threadbare jacket and brand-new jeans.

"It's a fucking racket," Lennon replied, laying on the thickest brogue he could muster. He sipped his drink, which was Sprite.

"I didn't catch your name."

"Ah, me?" Lennon asked. "Donal. Donal Stark."

Donald Westlake was one of Lennon's favorite crime writers, but he enjoyed Westlake's pseudonym, Richard Stark, even more.

"What happened . . . if you don't mind me asking."

"Auto wreck. My face took the worst of it."

"It looks painful."

"You know, after a few of these motherfookers, it feels just fine."

"That accent . . . you from Galway?" Trying to sound all worldly-like.

"Listowel, actually." Fucking Galway?

"Yeah, I thought so. You must be new at the *Welcomat*."

Lennon nodded. "Ah, yeah."

"I've been at the *City Press* for two years. They still got me stuck fact-checking restaurant listings. You know, if I had graduated five years earlier, dot coms would have been lining up to suck my dick."

"Terrible times, these are."

Despite the accent, Lennon tried to be boring enough to make his new friend seek conversation with someone else. Someone with ovaries, presumably. Women seemed to be at a premium at this gathering.

Speaking of which.

Lennon strolled over to check on Katie's progress.

Katie had spotted the drunk kid in the kitchen right away, and a plan was formed. She had gone over, made nice, helped him fill up his tumbler with ice cubes—slippery little suckers were sliding all over the place. Then she located an elusive bottle of Johnnie Walker Black that was tucked away, deep in a cabinet, where the party's hosts assumed the guests wouldn't dare venture. The kid, a real boyish-looking guy with curly black hair and delicate features, wore a wrinkled seersucker suit, and kept his line of sight on Katie's breasts, then hips, then eyes, thinking all the time that he was artfully stealing glances at the first two. His name was Will.

"What d'you do?" Will asked.

"You, later," Katie whispered, pouring more Johnnie Walker into his glass.

"No, I meant for a liv—," he started, then stopped himself. "Come again?"

Good God. This was going to take all night.

The plan: find some drunk blaggard, get him drunker, then usher him out, draped over their shoulders. The cops were looking for one or two male bandits, not a threesome.

The plan became trickier when Lennon overheard someone say, "Hey, chief. What's with the lights outside?"

Fucking hell.

"Seems we have some escaped bank robbers in the building," the chief said.

This was un-fucking-believable. About as un-fucking-believable as the rest of Lennon's weekend. This shit did not happen to professionals—this was fodder for those *America's Dumbest Criminals* books.

"Say what?"

"Yo—somebody get Will. We've got his next crime box, right here."

"Yes," the chief continued. "I got a call twenty minutes ago— one of our retired badges works the security detail downstairs. He thinks he spotted two of the guys who pulled that 211 at Wachovia yesterday."

"That two-what?" someone asked.

This was really un-fucking-believable.

"Police code for bank robbery, Ben."

"Yo, Will! Come on, man, get out here!"

Will.

Will was the drunk guy Katie was trying to sauce up. Their escape hatch. The compiler of a "crime box."

"What did the robbers get away with yesterday, anyway?"

"The bank president told me himself that it was $650,000.

Probably the biggest pinch around here in a while. But you didn't hear that from me."

"Shit. That's almost as much as Feldman paid for this place." There were nervous titters of laughter.

"Fuck that—you know how much these Rittenhouse condos run? Don't you keep up with *Metropolitan* magazine? You'd have to pull two of those Wachovia jobs to snag a pad like this."

Lennon walked by Katie close enough to whisper one word.

Gardai.

Police.

Fugitive

or

Prisoner

NO ONE NOTICED THEM LEAVE—THE PARTY WAS ALL the hell over the place, especially after the news spread that the John Dillinger gang was loose in the building. The elevator ride down was uneventful, too. There were uniforms everywhere, but no one seemed to want to bother with a man dressed in a clearly expensive Italian suit and a woman in a Vera Wang dress.

Two cops did, however, want to check the identity of the man slumped between them. Yeah, him. The unconscious one.

"We found this *boy* in the elevator," Katie said, her eyes crinkled up. "I didn't know that our building hosted frat parties from time to time."

"What's his name?"

"His name?" asked Katie. "Officer, I don't even know his eye color—he's out cold."

Will was out cold because after Katie had lured him into the hallway, Lennon had punched him twice in the head.

"Okay, ma'am, relax."

"Jesus—what happened to your face?" asked the other cop, who was staring at Lennon.

Lennon ignored him.

"Sarkissian—check the kid's ID."

One of the two uniforms reached around and fished a wallet out of Will's back pocket. He flipped it open, rolled his eyes, and whistled. "Shit. You're not going to believe this."

"What, already?"

"This frat boy is Will Issenberg."

"The crime box guy? The asshole who wrote about Murph—"

The first uniform—Sarkissian—turned back to Lennon and Katie. "Ma'am, we're sorry for the inconvenience. We'll take care of Mr. Issenberg from here. Just check in with Mr. Kotkiewicz at the front desk before you go, okay?"

Mr. Kotkiewicz at the front desk was a kindly-looking guy in his fifties. "I'm really sorry about all of this," he said, sliding a piece of paper and a pen toward them. "I just need you to write your names and apartment number on this log sheet."

"This really is turning into a terrorist state, isn't it?" Katie asked.

"I'll also need you both to put your hands flat on the counter and spread your legs."

Mr. Kotkiewicz was leveling a pistol at them.

"What is this?" Katie asked. She was also reaching up under Lennon's jacket to grab his Sig Sauer.

"Now!" Kotkiewicz shouted, stepping back. "Hands on the counter!"

The entire lobby—about a half-dozen cops, and a half-dozen

citizens—jolted. Guns were drawn, safeties clicked off. A uniform ran up behind Katie, hand on his holster.

But he was too slow.

Katie reached back and shoved the Sig Sauer up under his chin. He didn't look surprised, more resigned.

"We're walking out of here," Katie said. "You're going to let us go, and then we're going to let him go." With the word "him," she poked her hostage with the gun.

"No," said Kotkiewicz. "You're not going anywhere."

"I think this man here would disagree with you."

Lennon tried to process everything at once. The variables, the possible outcomes. Katie had done the right thing. If Lennon had reached for the gun, Kotkiewicz would have blasted first. But taking another cop hostage had taken things up a notch. Granted, it was a sound strategic move. That was Katie's strength—planning—but in the abstract. Never in the moment. She'd never been along for any jobs. She'd never been tagged for a crime. Ever. They'd had two very different childhoods.

Five seconds, and already she was staring at only two possible outcomes: fugitive or prisoner.

His sister. Mother of his unborn nephew/niece.

Push that shite away, Lennon thought. There were piles of problems in the world, but they could only be dealt with one at a time. Solve this one *now*.

Getting out the door wasn't the problem. The cops knew to stand down in a hostage situation—or at the very least, wait for a clean shot. Well, Lennon would be fucked if he was going to give them one. He walked behind Katie, reached around, and grabbed the hostage cop's gun. The two men formed a Katie sandwich, one in front, one behind. They slowly moved toward the front doors.

Revolving.

Fuck.

Move to the side. Hit the handicapped exit doors.

"Don't make a move, Patrick," Kotkiewicz said.

Fucker knew his name.

Probably tagged him from his I.O. on the way in here.

Think. *Solve.*

I just need a car, Lennon thought. I'm not good with armed stickups, or note jobs, or escapes from banks, or pipes, or with hostages, or any of that shite. I'm good with a car. If I can just get Katie into a car, and me behind the wheel, we have a chance.

The car was around the block.

Crime

Box

Guy

WILL ISSENBERG WAS NEVER RENDERED COMPLETELY unconscious. Shock had put him into a slightly vegetative state. With the first blow to the head, everything took on a numb, dreamlike quality, which reminded him of the first time he smoked pot. His IQ instantly lowered at least twenty-five points. And then with the second blow, another twenty-five points.

But he never lost consciousness.

So he heard everything, felt everything, and tried to keep reminding himself: remember this stuff. This is going to be great for the crime box. Remember what was said, and how it was said. Who did what and when.

Who, what, when, where, why. The basics.

This was going to be great. Just stay awake, and keep recording.

The only problem was that, lying there on the carpet in the moments after the shooting, Will couldn't remember one key detail: *Who fired first?*

When the shooting started, Will's eyes snapped open. Ostensibly, he saw the whole thing. But he couldn't get the action straight in his head. In the moment, the sound of bullets and snicks and pops and shattering glass and nicks seemed to fill the lobby, immediately followed by screams and a lone, hollow moan. Who fired at whom? In what order? Who was struck first? When did the windows shatter?

Blasts.

Bullets.

Smoke.

Screams.

Guns.

You try to figure out what the hell happened.

The only solid facts Will could trust were the end results, which was all he ever had when compiling his crime boxes for the *City Press*. Fat lot of good it did being an on-the-scene reporter. Which is when Will decided that maybe he had been wrong all of these years. Maybe he didn't love crime reporting so much. Maybe what he really liked were the end results, neatly compiled in the police logbooks, or in legal briefs. Those were solid, understandable, safe, distant. A writer could wrap his brain around things like that.

Live, on-the-scene reporting? That was bullshit. Schroedinger and his dead cat were right. You can't observe something without changing it.

Or it changing you.

This is what Will Issenberg thought about as his lungs collapsed, and he started to lose consciousness for real.

Free

"RELAX, SWEETIE," HE SAID. "JUST KEEP BREATHING."
They were temporarily stopped at a red light deep
in Southwest Philly. Lennon's left hand was on the wheel of
the stolen car; his right held a torn scrap of his jacket to Katie's
stomach.

SUNDAY a.m.

I am spending your money to have you and your family killed. Nice, eh?

— GEORGE "MACHINE GUN" KELLY

Relaxing with the Paper

SAUGHERTY READ ABOUT HIMSELF EARLY SUNDAY morning, not long after his ex-colleagues from the Philadelphia Police Department showed up for the third time to hear his story.

You know the story. The one about how his house got invaded and torched by niggers as well as his ex-boss, Lt. Earl Mothers, all of whom just so happened to perish in the blaze, leaving Saugherty alive to pursue another black gangster into South Philly, where he was brutally assaulted by—are you getting all of this?—a hanger-on of what remained of the Italian mob, and left broken and bleeding in an alley behind a restaurant.

Three cracked ribs, broken wrist, broken blood vessels up and down his face, two snapped fingers, internal bruising, and covered in gasoline. Saugherty thought that the gasoline was just gratuitous. As if to scare him. As if the broken parts weren't scary enough.

By the third visit, Saugherty was getting the idea that he was the number one suspect in the mysterious death of Lt. Earl Mothers. Internal Affairs was all over this like white on rice. They sniffed a shady deal gone wrong, somewhere. Mothers was not without splotches of mud on his record. Neither was Saugherty.

Amazingly, that wasn't the first article to catch Saugherty's attention Sunday morning.

It was another one: "Ex-Cop, Reporter, Killed in Shoot-out with Robbers."

Saugherty had almost skipped it at first, but the word *robber* nagged at him. He skimmed the first paragraph and the name practically jumped off the page and smacked him in the face.

Patrick Selway Lennon.

And an "unidentified female accomplice."

Saugherty couldn't believe what he was reading. The cops had somehow cornered two of the Wachovia heisters—Lennon, and this fuckup named Holden Richards—at the Rittenhouse Towers, one of the glitziest condos in Philly. Police found Richards upstairs, handcuffed to a pole.

But Lennon and his mysterious female accomplice crashed a party, then tried to sneak out with one of the guests, a two-bit crime hack named Will Issenberg. An ex-cop named Johnny Kotkiewicz made the ID and tried to arrest Lennon, but his accomplice took another cop hostage, and tried to make for the door. That's when the shooting started.

Lennon shot first, the paper said.

In the end, Issenberg bought it when a bullet hit his back and collapsed a lung. Kotkiewicz was shot in the throat, and died at the scene. No other officers or civilians were wounded.

Police believed that either Lennon, his accomplice, or possibly both were injured as they fled the scene in a stolen squad car. Pursuing officers lost the pair in a chase that extended from Rittenhouse Square deep into West Philly.

The third Wachovia suspect, Harrison Crosby, was also still at large.

Saugherty lowered the paper, and for the first time all night and morning, was filled with a gleeful kind of hope. The kind of hope that made the runny eggs and industrial-rubber sausage on his hospital tray seem edible.

The money was still out there.

Lennon wouldn't be going through all this shit if the money

wasn't still out there, somewhere. Richards obviously didn't know where it was, because his dumb white ass was now in the Gray Bar Hotel. This Crosby guy might be holding the loot bag, but even so, he still had to be in the city. Because Lennon was still in the city.

And the money was still in the city.

Saugherty decided maybe it was worth getting out of bed after all.

The Closet and the Mattress

THE DOOR SLAMMED. LISA JOLTED AWAKE IN THE CLOSET. Somebody else was here. Probably the doctor they had called a few hours ago.

At long fucking last.

Lisa had heard the whole thing.

She had been asleep on the mattress the night before when they came back in the early hours, the mystery guy and his girlfriend. Lisa thought she would just be confronting the guy, asking him what the hell he was doing here, but it didn't turn out that way. Besides, it sounded like both of them were hurt; she could hear it in their quiet gasps and moans.

When Lisa heard them walking up the carpeted staircase, the

wooden floor beneath them creaking from the weight, she came to her senses and scrambled across the floor and into the bedroom closet.

They entered the room just as she was easing the closet door shut.

"Take it easy," someone said. The mystery guy.

"I'll be okay." His female companion. "Where are you hit?"

"It doesn't matter. Wait . . . there's a mattress here on the floor. Ease down onto it. Keep pressure on your belly."

"It's just grazed," she said.

"You have an M.D. now? Lie back."

"Don't worry. The baby is fine. I can feel that much."

"It's not the baby I'm worried about."

Lisa cracked open the closet door a fraction of an inch. The room was dark, but she saw the outline of a man lowering a woman onto the mattress on the floor.

She could tell they were a couple—aside from the fact that the woman was apparently pregnant—because they bickered so much. Neither wanted to admit they were hurting, and both wanted to attend to the other's wounds. The mystery guy seemed to have the upper hand, though, because he had the number of a doctor scribbled on a napkin. The tide turned when Lisa heard that the woman was the one with the cell phone, and she insisted on making the call.

"He won't know you," the guy said.

"Who is he, anyway?" she asked.

"He came with the house."

"And where did the house come from?"

When Lisa heard the mystery guy tell the abbreviated story, she almost put a foot through the drywall in the closet.

The mystery guy didn't mention names, but he said that an Italian gentleman had agreed to let him use the house in exchange for half of "the take." The house came with guns, a set of clothes, and an unlicensed doctor to take care of injuries.

"Wait—you needed a doctor before tonight?" the woman asked.

"Not really."

"What do you mean, not really?"

"We were ambushed in the getaway car, then stripped and thrown into body bags. I woke up as two assholes were trying to shove me down a pipe, down by the river. Later I was shot. But I'm feeling much better."

"You were shot? By the Russians?"

"No. But the guys from earlier . . . one of them was Russian. The other was a college kid. Not Russian. American."

"Are they still out there?" the woman asked. "Will they be coming after us?"

"No," the guy said, quietly.

Lisa turned this over in her brain. A Russian. And a college kid. Mikal. And Andrew.

This is why she almost kicked the wall in.

"So let me call the doctor. Have him look at us both. And then we can get the fuck out of this city. We need to regroup."

"We need to talk," the woman said. "I have a lot to explain."

There was no torture greater than Lisa's hours in that closet, trapped, enveloped with rage. Right out of her closet door was the man who had killed her boyfriend. And the salt on that particular wound was the fact that her own father was this guy's partner in crime. Her dad had given them the use of this house! Her house! Her and Andrew's house! And guns. And clothes. And a doctor.

Lisa seethed as she listened to the phone call. She even knew the doctor they were calling. It was Dr. Bartholomew Dovaz, her own pediatrician. She had grown up afraid of Dr. Dovaz—he had an awful bedside manner, sticking you with needles when you weren't ready—until his wife got sick, and he started doing drugs. Lisa had assumed her family had severed all contact with Dr. Dovaz after a messy arrest in Lower Merion back in 1993, but apparently, her father had kept in touch with the man.

Her father had kept him on hand for special occasions. Like treating murderers he was hiding.

Had Lisa a weapon of any kind, she would have bolted from the closet and used it. Repeatedly. A gun. A baseball bat. A knife. A chainsaw. A nail gun. And then she'd confront her father later.

But she had nothing, and she had no idea what this couple was packing. They were professional criminals of some kind, and most likely had guns. Which made sense. They were talking about gunshot wounds. It would do no good to pop out of the closet and get shot in the head.

Lisa decided to wait for Dr. Dovaz to arrive, and then she'd figure out her move from there. There would be time to sneak away, to run back to her house and talk to her father.

She repeated things to herself, in her mind, so she could remember them later. They were important.

Getaway car.

Stripped, and thrown into body bags.

A pipe, down by the river.

A while later, Lisa fell asleep.

am

I

Blue

SAUGHERTY FELT WOEFULLY UNDERDRESSED TO BE calling on the Rittenhouse Towers on a Sunday morning.

He'd scraped together what he could. The clothes on his back from yesterday were ripped and blood-soaked; his house—and his pitiful wardrobe inside it—had probably burned to the ground.

That left one choice. Doctor's lounge. Saugherty knew his way around hospitals from his cop days, especially this one: Pennsylvania Hospital. He knew the ER. He knew the ER lounge, and how nobody really paid any attention to people popping in and out of it.

He found a pair of khakis and a nice black Eddie Bauer mock turtleneck in one of the lockers. He kept his own shoes, but glommed a shabby-looking black blazer from another locker. Didn't they pay these docs anything?

The Rittenhouse Towers were only twelve or so blocks away, across town, but since Saugherty had a busted arm, a sack full of broken ribs, and various other oochies and ouchies, he opted for a cab.

Getting in was not a problem; he knew the acting chief of security, Al Buchan, from his working the Fifteenth District. Saugherty fed him some line of bull about working a freelance bank robbery consulting thing for Lt. Earl Mothers, which Al swallowed without complaint. Let him up to 910, where a couple of uniforms told him he should check out 1809, where they hid out for a while.

"They" = Patrick Selway Lennon plus an unidentified female companion.

Saugherty got what he could from the guys on the scene; eyewitnesses weren't much use coming up with a name. The description was hazy, too. "Hot as balls," one guy had said, describing the unidentified female companion. "But an ice queen." Yeah, that helped. Saugherty poked around the condo, marveling at the appliances and utensils. The owner of the place, some guy named Feldman, even had a set of Tenmijurakus sitting on the counter. Swank.

It was getting to be that time, and the Percocets he got at the hospital were starting to lose their luster, so Saugherty found the appropriate cabinet, appropriated the appropriate bottle, then sequestered himself in the guest bathroom, near the entrance. Nothing fancy—just a bottle of Johnnie Walker. But when he closed the door behind him, Saugherty realized he'd hit the fucking lottery. It was Johnnie Walker *Blue*. He'd never tasted it; only read about it in the storybooks and musty volumes of Greek and Roman fables. Saugherty took this surprise as a good omen. With $650,000, he'd be able to enjoy J.W. Blue on a regular basis.

He unscrewed the cap and breathed in the smoky aroma through his nose. It was almost a contact high.

There was a dispenser of small plastic Dixie cups on the bathroom sink. Saugherty plucked one off the stack and poured himself a tall one, almost to the brim. This was not something to be sucked from the bottle, nor cut with tap water. Presentation was one thing.

The taste was everything else.

Saugherty sat on the closed toilet, in a frayed blazer not his own, drinking some incredibly fine Scotch that was not his own, either. For having woken up in a hospital bed and been grilled by humorless jackasses from Internal Affairs, he thought he was doing all right.

He let the liquid pleasantly burn down into his stomach, and felt the attitude-adjustment mechanisms turning in his brain. He lifted his face to heaven, by way of thanking God.

As his head returned to its usual forward-facing position, Saugherty spotted it.

The bathroom closet door, slightly ajar.

Saugherty didn't go to it right away. He wanted to finish the Scotch in his Dixie cup first, because he knew what he was going to find in there. The lead he needed. And once he found it, he would be leaving the bathroom, and tracking down more leads, and eventually, tracking down his money.

The morning had been so charmed, how could it be otherwise?

Ten minutes later, the bathroom closet yielded a small black suitcase. Which yielded a set of women's clothing and toiletries. And beneath that, identification and a passport.

Hiya, Katie Elizabeth Selway.

Paterfamilias

"SO WHO'S THE FATHER?"

"Mary, Mother of God," she said, sighing.

"You're not gonna tell me?"

"Yes, I'm going to tell you. But this isn't how I'd planned it."

"Ah. Right. Puerto Rico. He supposed to meet us there?"

"He's there right now."

"And why aren't you there now?"

"I got worried."

Lennon leaned his head back against the wall and shut his eyes. Katie was a few feet away, reclining on the mattress.

He didn't want to say it, but he'd told her a million times: no matter what, even if I'm arrested, don't come looking for me. I can take care of myself. That was Rule Number One. That had always been Rule Number One, ever since Lennon had reunited with his sister, and confessed to her what he did for a living. But Katie wasn't much for rules.

"Do I know him?"

"No . . . not really."

"So I fookin' do know him. What's his name?"

"Oh, Patrick."

"His first name, at least."

"You know, this *really* isn't the way I imagined this. I had Vueve Clicquot. I had reservations. I had it perfectly planned."

"Yeah, so did I."

They sat there in silence. Mulling things over. Waiting for the doctor to arrive. Sunlight was starting to creep around the cheap fabric window shades.

"I'm going to have to find that money," Lennon said, at long last.

"Why?"

"You're going to need a crib."

"Michael has . . . shit."

"Michael? Fucking Michael who?"

Lennon spun through his mental Rolodex of pro heisters, but nothing came to mind. Common enough name, Michael. But he really didn't know any. At least, he hadn't worked with any Michaels in the past few years. Had he? Unless it was that . . . nah. Couldn't be.

"Okay. Last name."

"Never you mind. Keep your mind on the money. You hate being distracted in the middle of a job, remember?"

"Too fookin' late for that."

"Come on, Patrick. Don't be a shithead. We can just walk away. Last time I balanced the checkbook, we were doing okay. This money was for the future."

"I have more immediate needs."

"Like what?"

"Like I need $350,000 to pay for this house and torn-up suit I'm wearing."

"It's a nice suit, but I think you paid too much for the house."

Lennon chuckled, in spite of himself. It broke the dam. He could be himself with his sister. She was the only person in the world he felt comfortable around.

So he told her everything that had happened since Friday morning—the double cross, the attempted burial at the pipe down by the river, the dorm, the car theft, the rogue cop, the gunshot wound, the threats, the black guys with guns, the burning house, the 7-Eleven heist, the parking lot, the meeting with the junior-grade Mafioso, the deal, the trip to Wilcoxson's condo. . . .

Lennon lapsed into Gaelic every so often, but Katie understood enough to follow. She had grown up in the U.S., and had a faint New England accent. Lennon had spent most of his time in Listowel, and then Dublin, before emigrating to the U.S., mostly to find his sister. Their parents had died years before.

"If you want the money, there's one thing you have to do."

"What's that?" Lennon asked.

"Go back to the pipe, and see who's buried there."

"You're thinking of Bling."

"I'm thinking of Bling."

Lennon sighed. "I'm not sure what I want more—to find his body, or not to find his body."

"I think you want to find his body."

That's when the doorbell rang. Dr. Bartholomew Dovaz was back for the second time in a twelve-hour period.

"I'll get it," Lennon said. "But as soon as he leaves, you're telling me which Michael defiled you."

Back
to
the
Pipe

WHEN DR. DOVAZ TOOK THE WOMAN INTO THE BATH-room, and the guy, Patrick, went downstairs to use the half bathroom, Lisa took the opportunity to split.

Things happened quickly after that.

Lisa's dad kept trying to yell at her, trying to be the father—*What the hell were you doing in that house? Is that your house?*—but Lisa wasn't hearing that. She kept pounding him with what she'd learned, over and over again. The guy is a murderer. He killed Andrew. He killed Mikal. He stuffed their bodies in a pipe down by the river. The guy is a murderer! He killed Andrew! He killed Mikal! He stuffed their bodies in a pipe down by the fucking river!

Eventually Lisa's dad saw the light of reason and assembled a team. It wasn't hard to find the pipe Lisa was talking about. There was only one major construction project down on the Delaware River. The new children's museum. Lisa's dad's team took shotguns, baseball bats, and baling hooks. They didn't need the first two items. Everybody inside the pipe was dead. They recovered six bodies before reaching mud and clay at the bottom of the pipe. Two of the faces matched a photo they were given, a black-and-white promotional photo of a band called Space Monkey Mafia. It was the bass player and the keyboard player.

The team knew the keyboard player. It was Lisa's boyfriend, Andrew.

Andrew didn't look too good. He had a black Bic pen sticking out of his neck. Blood had caked and dried all around it.

They called it in to Lisa's dad, and he told them to dump all the bodies down the pipe again. No questions; just do it. So they did.

"But before you do," Lisa's dad said, "take the pen out of the boy's neck. And bring it to me."

SUNDAY P.M.

I want you all to know that I don't take no orders.

— "BABY FACE" NELSON

Ink
and
Blood

WHEN LENNON WOKE UP AGAIN, HE WAS TIED TO A chair, and his throat was sore.

Other people were in the room. Which was not the room he'd fallen asleep in. The last thing he knew, he had been given a shot of painkillers. He didn't want the doctor to give him something that would render him unconscious. "Don't worry," the doctor had said. "This'll just take the edge off."

Lennon's vision focused a bit. He saw Katie in the corner of the room. Her hands were behind her back. She was wearing stark white lipstick, and her eyes looked puffed shut. Somebody held a gun to her head.

Now somebody slapped him in the face.

"Hi, Dillinger," a male voice said. He had said it the correct way—*Dill-ING-er*. Most people thought it was *dill-IN-jer*, like the pistol. "Glad you could join us."

Lennon tried to count the people in the room. Aside from his sister. He got up to five before somebody slapped him again.

"Stay with us," said the same voice. "This is important. This concerns you, and your pregnant girlfriend there."

Pregnant girlfriend my arse. Lennon wanted to shout it at the top of his lungs. He was tired of the charade. It was a handy charade—people assumed they were a couple, so let them think that. It made tracking them down all the more difficult. But that didn't really matter now, did it? They were already tracked down.

"What the fuck did you give him, Dovaz? Horse tranks?"

"I gave him what he required."

"Jesus. The guy's a fucking zombie."

"I'm not sure that's entirely the fault of my medication."

Another slap—harder this time. Lennon felt his teeth vibrate in his gums.

"You see this, Dillinger?"

Lennon focused. He saw a beefy hand holding a pen.

"You stuck this pen in a kid's neck a few days ago. You remember that?"

The hand clenched the pen tighter. Lennon could make out the crimson glaze that still caked it. Holy Jesus. This guy had been down in the pipe.

"That kid was my daughter's boyfriend."

Who knows, Lennon thought. Maybe he was your daughter's brother. It's not right to jump to conclusions like that.

"Are you going to say something, you mute bastard?"

Lennon opened his mouth, but nothing came out.

He was going to say: "Fuck you, ya cunt."

But he couldn't.

"Trying to talk, ain't ya? Well, you can't. For real now. I know you were playing me—my daughter told me she heard you talking. Those days are over, fucker."

Lennon tried again but felt razor blades churning around in his throat. What did that bastard do to me? he thought. His eyes snapped to the doctor—Dovaz—and saw a tiny smirk under his beard.

"Yeah, I had you fixed, Dillinger. The good doctor here was kind enough to help me out. He poured some acid down your throat there. So you're just going to sit there and listen to me."

Somebody else wheeled a tray into view. He was big and pasty-looking, with ugly tortoiseshell glasses and a bushy, greasy moustache hanging under his nose. Spread out on the top of the tray were all kinds of tools, surgical and otherwise—scalpels, hammers, wrenches, clamps, needles. There was dried blood on some of the tools. In the corner there was a folded-up set of leather stirrups.

"Nothing to retort? Good. You can listen up. I've got your girlfriend over there. Pretty soon, we're going to move her to an undisclosed location—just like Dick Cheney. Then, a little while later, we're going to set you free. I know, you're saying, no way, but we are. What you're going to do for me, Dillinger, is you're going to rob some banks. I figure you'll need to knock over at least one a day, because your girlfriend's room and board is going to be $5,000 a day. I read in a book that the average bank robber can only expect between two and three grand for your average note job. That's why I'm saying you're going to have to rob *at least* one a day."

Lennon stared at him.

"And I'll know if you're robbing banks or not. I read the *Daily News* every day—it's delivered right to my doorstep. They cover everything. Some guy takes a piss on the side of a building, it's in the paper the next day. So I'll be looking for your work."

What the fuck was this cunt talking about?

"You should probably get yourself a nickname. All the big bank robbers have them. The Bad Breath Bandit. The Zit-Face Bandit. The Bobby DeNiro Bandit. You can be the Oh Shit, I Got My Vocal Cords Burned Bandit. How's that? But really, you should figure out something. You want to be distinctive. Anyway, after you pull down the heist, you're going to deliver the money to this address, right here. You can keep a couple of bucks for yourself, just so you can get by. But a couple of my boys will be waiting for your delivery. You try anything, you'll be the Pushing Up Daisies Bandit. Swear to fucking God. And your woman here? She'll be the Girlfriend Who Had a Rusty Coat Hanger Abortion."

Lennon decided right then to make this man die slowly. He wasn't exactly sure of the details yet, but it didn't matter.

Once he had a goal fixed in his mind, the rest was academic.

"Yeah. See these tools here? Probably got you all nervous. Well, relax. They're not for you. They're for her. You fuck up, get arrested, try to fuck with us, or piss on the side of the wrong building, and we take it out on her. And the kid inside. We got all kinds of ways of pulling that little bastard of yours out. Don't worry. It won't survive long. She don't look that pregnant."

This bastard, Lennon decided, was going to die the slowest of slow deaths. The kind where you start out with a cheese grater and a blowtorch, and things escalate from there.

"Okay. That's it. You work for us until you pay back what you owe, and then we let her go on her way. You fuck up, she dies. And I send somebody to hunt you down, too. Whaddya think, Dillinger?"

Just for thinking the thoughts.

"I'll take your silence as agreement."

And then someone hit Lennon from behind. That failed to render him unconscious, as someone else quickly noted, so the first person hit him again, which did the trick.

MONDAY a.m.

This bank, my sister could have robbed.

— PATRICK MICHAEL MITCHELL

Breakfast in Bed

THE SAD TRUTH WAS THIS: LENNON WASN'T REALLY A bank robber. Sure, he'd taken part in countless bank heists. If you had handed him an application with a box that requested previous experience, and if you could somehow persuade Lennon to fill it out, he'd write "bank robber" in that box. But technically, Lennon had never robbed a single bank. He had merely transported bank robbers from one point (right outside the bank) to another point (another vehicle, or a safe house, or an airport, or a cave in the woods) in exchange for a cut of the money. Lennon was a master getaway driver. He'd read a ton about bank robberies. But still: he was not a bank robber.

So for his first solo robbery, Lennon picked the easiest target he could think of: a bank inside a supermarket. He'd read they were the easiest. Nobody wants to shop for doughnuts and cold cuts inside something that resembles Fort Knox.

His target: a SuperFresh on South Street, a long walk from the mob's safe house in South Philly. Lennon had stolen a car from a few blocks away, then simply driven up Ninth Street until he saw the supermarket. It was a start.

But Lennon had no intention of robbing banks for that fat Italian gobshite bastard. He just knew he had to put his hands on enough money to appease the goons left behind at the safe house, spend two dollars of it on a screwdriver, then use it to get some answers. Then collect Katie and finally get the fuck out of Philadelphia forever.

He didn't remember anything else useful from the previous night; the second blow had knocked him out cold. The next morning, Lennon had woken up alone in the same house, in the same bedroom, on the same mattress. He had tried out his voice; he still couldn't use it. He wondered if those drops Dovaz had used were permanent. Wouldn't that be a scream.

On the floor next to him was a typed note that read, "Eat breakfast and get going." There were three Nutri-Grain bars and a liter bottle of spring water. The note continued: "Make your daily deposit through the mail slot at 1810 Washington Ave."

So the bastard had been serious, after all. Rob banks, hand him the money.

That's when he saw that the note had been resting on something else—a piece of fabric.

No, not fabric—underwear.

Katie's.

Lennon drank some of the water—which burned the living shit out of his throat—then put the bars in his jacket pockets and left the house. He stole a car, then saw the SuperFresh a short while later. Let's get this over with already.

How the FBI Gets Its Man

BLING HAD ALWAYS BEEN THE BANK HEIST MASTER-mind, but he didn't talk shop too much. Just concrete details, like this joint here's got an ACU that sniffs gunpowder. Lennon would nod and file it away. All Lennon really had to know was that Bling knew his shit enough to be outside, with the money, no worries. Most of what Lennon knew about bank heists came from books he read as a kid in Ireland—stuff brought over by his American dad in a duffel bag. They were musty paperbacks with titles like *How the FBI Gets Its Man* and *The Bad Ones* and *We Are the Public Enemies* and *I, Mobster* and *New York: Confidential*. They sparked his adolescent imagination and led him to crime encyclopedias and lurid biographies and yellowed men's magazines he nicked from bookshops in Listowel.

Lennon always knew his father was a bad guy, but Lennon's mum never shared the details. She'd only spent a couple of weeks with him while on holiday in New York City in 1971. Freddy Selway made a few visits to see his boy later on, but only when he needed a place to hide overseas. It was during one of these visits, in 1979, that he'd brought along the duffel bag full of paperbacks. Freddy had to split, so he left the bag behind. Or maybe he'd left the bag behind on purpose. Lennon never knew. In late December

1980, Freddy Selway was killed trying to kill somebody else. Lennon's daddy was a hit man.

Lennon kept his father's paperbacks in a safe-deposit box in a small federal bank in Champaign, Illinois, along with $54,000 in emergency funds. The books were among his most prized possessions; he didn't dare leave them somewhere that might be compromised.

Right now, his mind kept coming back to *How the FBI Gets Its Man*. It was one of the many books produced by the FBI, under the watchful eye of J. Edgar Hoover, meant to glorify the agency. The bad guys were punished; the G-men were always smarter and sharper and quicker to their guns. But Lennon, even at a young age, identified with the heisters and killers, who had cool names and led interesting lives. Lives he imagined his father leading.

He knew all about bank robbery from *How the FBI Gets Its Man*.

There were lone-wolf note jobs, and multiple-man takeover teams. Since Lennon lacked a team and a voice, a takeover was out. It had to be a note job. Quick and clean. He also knew that bank tellers were instructed to cooperate with bank robbers no matter what, lest the bank robber go crazy and start pumping the clientele full of lead. So the key was the note. The note had to be fucking *scary*. So scary, the teller had to think twice about an alarm, or a dye pack, or any other bullshit.

This is why Lennon thought a bank inside a supermarket was his best bet. There were moms and kids and old people and all kinds of innocent bystanders, there to buy milk and bread and juice and cereal. No teller was going to argue with a scary man with a gun.

Fuck. A gun.

He'd have to fake that. . . .

No. Wait.

This was America, post–9/11. He'd only have to fake a bomb.

Here's a Suggestion

LENNON STOPPED INSIDE A MCDONALD'S AND BOUGHT A nine-pack of Chicken McNuggets—easy protein—with change he'd found in the stolen car. He sat down and wrote his note, using a pen ripped from the "Give Us Your Suggestions!" box and the back of a McDonald's job application. When he finished eating his chicken, Lennon borrowed the gold token that would unlock the bathroom, where he used water to pat down his hair and straighten his tie and lapels and try to look as respectable as possible. Which was tough, seeing that his face bore the bruises and scrapes of a rough beating.

What the hell. Maybe that added to his scary factor.

Before stopping at McDonald's, Lennon had walked into a junk shop and pocketed a plastic beeper toy meant for a toddler. God knows why toddlers needed to play with beepers, but that was something for Katie to figure out later. With Michael. Whoever the fuck Michael was.

Next stop: a Mailboxes, Etc., where he nicked a package in a metal bin meant for Herman Wolf in Warminster, Pennsylvania. Sorry, Herman. It was the right size.

On to SuperFresh.

Lennon flashed back to his favorite chapter from *How the FBI Gets Its Man*—chapter 7, which was a short history of Al Nussbaum, genius bank robber. Nussbaum kept a farm in upstate New York full of high-powered weaponry and bomb-making materials. He was the man who, in the mid-1960s, pioneered the idea that a mad bomber epidemic could distract police from bank heists going down.

Nussbaum probably never had to worry about stealing toy beepers or packages from mail services.

SuperFresh was like every other American supermarket he'd visited—bright, cool, crisp, white, frigid, and overstuffed with food neatly packed into every conceivable shelf, corner, and aisle.

Lennon placed the bomb on top of a stack of Fruity Pebbles—on sale for $3.99 this week—then walked over to the bank teller. He waited his turn, then slid the note across the Formica countertop.

Peanut
Butter

SOMETHING ON THE SCANNER CAUGHT SAUGHERTY'S ear—a bit about a dead woman. A bunch of kids found her in an abandoned lot in Southwest Philly where neighborhood residents dump old furniture and trash.

Saugherty had holed himself up in the Comfort Inn up in Bensalem, right off Route 1, just out of the city limits. He took a corner room so he could see the highway. He didn't want the flashing cherries and blueberries to come screaming out of nowhere. He was still under investigation, as far as he knew. He hadn't made himself reachable.

The room was packed with the necessary supplies: the police scanner, of course, to see if his Irish bank-robber buddy had emerged. Two sixes of Yuengling Lager in a hard-case cooler. Three bottles of Early Times. A bottle of Jack Daniel's. Two bottles of Ketel One—a buddy of his had turned him on to that stuff. Sipping vodka. Go figure. Six bottles of water. Two sticks of pepperoni; one block of sharp white cheese. Box of Ritz. Rye bread, liverwurst, mustard, fat red onion. He stuck the liverwurst and sharp cheese in the cooler with the beer. The rest could stay out. He'd also paid a visit to his private armory over in Tacony, along the river. There was a bunch of stuff in a black canvas bag under the bed.

Saugherty had been listening for key words like "bank robber" or "heist" or "Wachovia" or "Lennon," but then caught the police code for body dump. He called a friend on the force and asked for the skinny, which was: woman, late twenties, found naked at Forty-ninth and Grays Ferry, her wrists and ankles bound with brown extension cords and her body smeared with peanut butter. She was three months pregnant.

Wait, back up, said Saugherty. Peanut butter.

Yeah, confirmed the source. Peanut butter. People on the scene thought the killer—or dumper—smeared it on so rats from the area would eat the evidence.

You got a photo? asked Saugherty. Something nagged him about this.

After some back and forth, the source agreed to fax a photo of the woman's face over to the Comfort Inn's business center. Saugherty took another three sips of Early Times, then wandered down there.

He got the faxed photo.

Holy fucking shit.

Superfucked

I *HAVE A BOMB IN A PACKAGE IN ONE OF THE AISLES. GIVE me all your money—no dye packs, no alarms—or people will die.*
No sense fucking around with it, Lennon thought. This wasn't

an essay for a cash prize; this was a bank robbery demand note. He'd never written one before, but he surmised the most successful were direct and to the point.

The girl across the counter looked down at the note. She was pretty, in a geeky kind of way. Her brown hair was cut unflatteringly and she wore chunky glasses that her Goth friends probably thought were cool. But Lennon liked her look. He didn't like that he was going to cause her some major grief this morning. This is why he enjoyed getaway driving: no personal interaction, no countermeasures, none of this at all.

She looked up at him questioningly. Are you serious?

Lennon froze his face, deadpan. Yes, I'm fucking serious. He let her see the toy beeper in his hand.

The girl nodded, then started to busy herself under the counter. Lennon waited.

"We're supposed to put a security packet in here," she said, quietly. "But I'm not going to do that. I want you to know that, okay?"

Lennon nodded.

"It's not much, either. Just a little over a thousand. But I'm not holding back."

Lennon blinked at her. Come on, love.

"Just don't hurt anybody, okay?"

Enough was enough already. He raised the toy beeper.

The girl slid him the money, tucked in a white plastic bag. She hadn't asked if he'd wanted paper.

Lennon took the bag and walked toward the exit. There was a little boy trying to rattle a prize out of a small red machine in the aisle and a young couple pushing a cart full of bagged groceries. He stepped around them and through the automatic doors, which whooshed open at his approach. Through the vestibule, to the other set of doors.

Which refused to open.

As did the ones behind him, when he backed up. The young couple looked at him through the glass. What did you do?

Oh, fuck me, he thought.

Trapped.

Like a gerbil in a Habitrail.

At that moment, for the first time all weekend, Lennon was glad Bling had been killed. He wasn't sure how he would have explained this to him.

A short while later, after the police had arrived and Lennon was in cuffs and ready to be led to the nearest squad car, the girl from the grocery store approached him. She looked at him through those clunky glasses like a curious schoolgirl at a science exhibit.

"Next time," she said, "pick a toy beeper that doesn't say Fisher-Price on the side."

She didn't actually say that. Lennon imagined her saying that. Because that's how this story was going to end, when it was written up for the newspapers in a couple of hours. The bomb angle, the toy. Guaranteed coverage. And the early editions would wrap up a little after midnight, and sooner or later, a copy would wind up in that Italian bastard's hands, and Katie would be killed.

The

Second

Fax

LEAVE ME THE HELL ALONE ALREADY," HIS SOURCE whined.

"Come on. One lousy photo."

"What, are you whacking off to crime photos over there? It's just some stupid asshole who tried to knock over a bank with a phony beeper and a napkin from McDonald's. Happens every day. Read all about it in tomorrow's *Daily News.*"

"Come on. One lousy fuckin' photo, Jonsey."

"Am I bent over a desk? Are you tickling my colon, you asshole?"

"Come *on.*"

"You're a son of a bitch, Saugherty."

"I know, I know. You need the fax number again?"

A few minutes later, Saugherty knew that the Philadelphia Police Department had captured Patrick Selway Lennon, only they didn't know it yet—unless the cops involved in Saturday night's shoot-out happened to drop by the holding cell. Not likely. The buzzword on the Philly P.D.: understaffed, overwhelmed. The mayor had just whacked 1,400 jobs—among them, cops and firemen—from the city payrolls the previous winter. They made the best of what they had. The Wanted posters from Saturday night hadn't even circulated, and the fingerprint hit wouldn't come back for about an hour. If they could get to it.

Which gave him about an hour.

Shit. He'd barely recovered from the shock of the first fax and gotten another few sips of Early Times in when the scanner said something about a 211 down on South Street. Which made no sense whatsoever, but the last place Saugherty had seen Lennon had been only a few blocks south of South, at the Italian joint. So it did make a kind of cockeyed sense. Plus, his gut twitched the same way it had before. This was something.

He'd have to leave this tumbler of Early Times behind. Breakfast would have to wait.

Saugherty hopped in his stolen car and drove down Cottman, hooked a left onto Princeton, hopped on I-95, and hoped the morning traffic snarls had figured themselves out. The roundhouse was all the way downtown, and he couldn't be late. He had another quick stop first. He had a bag to pick up.

MONDAY P.M.

To a few, it'll be grief
To the law, a relief
But it's death for Bonnie and Clyde.

— BONNIE PARKER

any
Goodly
amount

FIRST OF ALL, YOU CAN CUT THE SHIT ABOUT BEING mute. I KNOW you're not, okay?"

Saugherty had tap-danced like Fred Astaire on uppers to get inside this interrogation room. And this mick bastard was still playing the Shields and Darnell shit.

"Just say hi, you asshole. We don't have time for this."

The bank robber stared at him, his eyes opened wide, as if he was trying to mentally communicate with Saugherty. His hands were cuffed behind his back, looped through the chair. Go ahead and threaten to detonate a bomb in the U.S., see what happens. Saugherty still couldn't believe he was in here.

Now the guy was trying to mouth something.

"I can't read lips, so quit it. Do-you-know-where-the-money-is?"

The guy sighed.

Saugherty wanted to crawl up the side of the room and shit nickels. But then he stopped. Had he made a mistake? Was it possible the guy didn't actually speak before firing that gun and blowing up Saugherty's garage? Did he imagine the whole thing? No. He had heard it. That Irish brogue, the word "arsehole," as if asshole needed the extra consonant. So what was going on here?

"Let me make it plain. I-know-where-your-sister-is."

The bank robber's eyes snapped to attention.

"Yeah, I know she's your sister. Katie Selway. I know she got caught up in this whole thing, and I know she's in trouble. And I can help you get to her."

Of course, Saugherty was completely fumbling around this one. And he had left out an important detail or two, but that could be ironed out later.

"That got your attention, didn't it?"

The guy nodded. Slightly. As if to say, go on.

"I need to know you're going to help me out at the end of this, then. We need to recover that money, and then I'll help you recover your sister. Do we have an agreement?"

Lennon, the bank robber, actually seemed to be thinking it over. He knew where the money was, alright.

He nodded again. Just once.

"You know, we have the most revealing conversations, you and I," Saugherty said. "I love that about us. In this business, it's really hard to meet people you feel a connection with. Do you feel the same way? Okay. Get ready."

The two men sat there in the soft pink room with the wire mesh on the opaque windows, getting ready.

"It's about to go off."

Silence.

"What's about to go off, you ask? The suitcase nuke I put in a locker over at the bus station at Tenth and Filbert. Let's go."

I-95

THE EX-COP WAS A LUNATIC LOSER. BUT THEN AGAIN, Lennon had been sitting in a cell, plotting an escape, a way out, a way back to Katie, and he'd come up with nothing better.

Lennon needed to reach Katie if he did nothing else on this earth before he left it. So let the ex-cop's greed lead the way. Lennon didn't know where the Wachovia money was any more than he knew the location of the Holy Fucking Grail. But this ex-cop, Saugherty, didn't need to know that yet. And dealing with one ex-cop was better than a stationhouse full of full-time police officers.

Besides, an extra man would come in handy when he went to the drop-off point and made those Italian fucks tell him about Katie. He could always just tell . . . or write, that is . . . Saugherty that this mob capo, Perelli, had the money. And they had to go through Perelli to get it back. Problem solved. Saugherty could be dealt with later.

Amazingly, no one gave a fuck when they just walked out the front door. Saugherty fed them some bullshit about "transferring the prisoner," and that was it. No fuss, no muss. No one had identified him as the same guy who was taking shots at some cops over at Rittenhouse Square two nights before. Nobody blinked. Was this city for real? This guy Saugherty just flashed some old piece of plastic ID and they were out of there. Into a car. A blue Chevrolet Cavalier. They both climbed in without a word. Saugherty took them up one street, then turned right, blurring past some brick buildings with historical designations on them, then they were on I-95, headed north. America.

"Okay, you're officially sprung. You can cut the shit and start talking."

Oh Jesus. Here we go again.

"Look, you mick bastard. I know you can speak. I heard you. Right before you blew up my fucking house. You said something about arseholes. Which I really fucking love. The extra 'r' in there. Why not just say asshole? No fucking idea."

Lennon, of course, said nothing. He couldn't. Not that this cop would understand that. Just let him keep flapping his gums. It was more time to figure out a next move.

"Still the tough guy, eh? Look, really, cut it the fuck out. We need each other, otherwise you wouldn't even be here. Here's the deal. I'm taking us up to my hotel room. Now don't get that look on your face. I'm not a fag. You're not my type, anyway. I like men who can moan when I fuck them up the ass. Most you could do is scratch on the mattress. And frankly, that wouldn't do it for me. It's all about the audio."

The white lane markers whizzed by at seventy miles per hour.

"Christ, you're a humorless fuck."

Lennon saw the city receding behind him and realized they were headed north. Or northeast. To the Northeast. Where this ex-cop used to live. If Katie were anywhere, she'd be south of the city, where those Italians operated.

He opened the glove compartment and a .38 snub-nosed revolver popped out. Lennon saw Saugherty's eyes bug for a moment, but Lennon put up his palms to say, easy, now, not going for the blaster. With two fingers, he picked the gun up by the trigger guard and placed it on his lap. Then he rooted around until he found what he wanted: a pen and a stack of fast-food napkins. Well, the napkins weren't exactly what he wanted, but it would do.

Find my sister, he wrote, and showed it to Saugherty.

"No, sorry," the ex-cop said. "We gotta go back and get ready. We need hardware, and you need a fresh set of clothes. I need to finish my Early Times, even though the ice is probably all melted. Then we talk about the money."

Lennon put the .38 to Saugherty's head.

"It's not loaded," Saugherty said.

Lennon dry-clicked.

"See?"

Carrying
Charge

WHEN THEY GOT BACK TO THE HOTEL, SAUGHERTY had to change his tighty-whiteys. He hadn't actually known if that .38 had been loaded or unloaded; he'd borrowed the Cavalier from his bookie after his own car got torched. Could that Irish bastard tell the gun was unloaded from the weight? Who knew.

Lennon sat down in a chair by the window while Saugherty fished around in the black bag under his bed. He knew he had a spare set of clothes here somewh . . . yeah, here they were. Something he had filched from a drug dealer in Kensington. He threw the white bundle in Lennon's lap.

It was a white tracksuit with gold piping. The logo on the front read, "I'm the Daddy."

You've got to be fucking joking, said the look on Lennon's face.

"Hey, least it doesn't smell funny. Go ahead. Take a shower while you're at it—you need one. I'll get us some food. You want a drink?"

Lennon nodded and stood up.

"I've got Early Times, some fancy vodka, a bottle of Jack—"

Lennon nodded on the "Jack."

"Jack? Coming right up. Neat or on the rocks? You're probably a neat guy. I've got some liverwurst here, too. You in the mood for a sandwich? Probably. You don't get a meal in the clink until late evening. I'll make you one, hold the onion. You don't need onion."

By that time, Lennon was already in the shower.

Saugherty did some hard thinking. There were a lot of fancy ways around this; make this bank robber guy play along until he dug up the heist money. But why? Saugherty was honestly tired of thinking so damn much. His life usually ended up in shambles when he tried to get too cute. He looked over at the dresser and fished the faxed photo of the dead woman out of the pile.

The dead woman named Katie Elizabeth Selway.

No, no time to be cute. Let's give honesty a spin, see where it takes us.

Right?

Hmm.

No.

No fucking way.

We gotta keep lying.

Saugherty pushed the faxed photo back into the stack. He scooped a handful of ice from the cooler to freshen up his Early Times, swirled it around, and drained the tumbler. Then more ice, more Early Times. He could use some coffee with this, to even things out. Food, too, though suddenly, he wasn't in the mood for liverwurst sandwiches. Saugherty craved a Big Mac and large fries—cop food, his old drive-thru favorite. He knew he was somewhere in the twilight between a hangover and the next good hard drunk, and he had to stay there for a while. Maintain. Food would help him do that. Wait until this stuff was settled.

He needed to think.

"I'm going out for five minutes," he called through the bathroom door. "I'd ask if you needed anything, but what would be the point, right?"

Stacks o' Fax

LENNON SAT DOWN AT THE DESK AND IGNORED THE LIVerwurst sandwich. Instead he sipped his Jack. Not his usual drink—he enjoyed a good single malt when he was kicking back off the job. Even a little Jameson to cap off an evening. But it would do. Jack was in the same liquor family. And as far as being on or off the job, who knew? At some point he had crossed a line. The job had formally ended. This was recovery.

On the desk was a stack of file folders. Lennon took the top one and flipped it open. A police report. Interview with a suspect, a thermal fax of fingerprints, then pages of typed transcript. What was this stuff?

Saugherty was a cop—or an ex-cop. He knew that much. Was this stuff freelance? He started thumbing through the pages to kill time. A lot of stuff on drug dealers. Transcripts, evidence photos. Not just one case, either. A bunch of them, scrambled together.

There was a photo here. A guy in dreadlocks with scars all over his forehead and cheeks. Looked like Seal's uglier cousin.

Another photo: a young woman with mousy hair and a weak chin. Even though the picture was black and white, her eyes looked like they glowed.

Another photo still: an older man. Bony and gray-haired. Looked like Terence Stamp. If Terence Stamp needed a shave and a hug.

Another photo . . .

Target
Bag

SAUGHERTY KEYED BACK INTO THE HOTEL ROOM, mouth full OF Mickey D's French fries, then for the second time that day nearly defiled himself.

The image before him unpacked itself in a fragmented, Dick-and-Jane style in Saugherty's brain. See Lennon. See Lennon look at faxed crime photos. See Lennon look at dead Katie Elizabeth Selway photo.

See Lennon snap Saugherty's neck.

The mute looked up at him. And while he didn't smile, the way he curled his lip indicated to Saugherty that all was cool. Lennon didn't know yet. If he had, it would have been obvious in his eyes. What's more, Lennon would have probably gut-shot him where he stood. Saugherty would have bled to death with a face full of fries.

"Hey," he said.

Lennon nodded, then turned back to the stack of papers.

"Got you a grilled McChicken sandwich. Figured you were into this Atkins shit, from the looks of you."

Pause. Maybe he wasn't Atkins after all. Maybe he should've bought the guy a Quarter Pounder. Or a Happy Meal.

Spin, Saugherty, Spin.

"What you're looking at there is the sad remnants of a career in law enforcement. Yeah, it's true. Took it right from the filing cabinets down at the roundhouse. No one cared. Everything fit into a plastic bag from Target. Walked them right out of there."

Lennon was still flipping, idly.

"Thing is, my ex-partner was crooked. What you have in front of you there is the remnants of hundreds of broken lives." Huh. That sounded good, Saugherty thought. "Planted evidence. Rigged trials. You name it. And the day he painted the inside of his Ford

Explorer with his brains was the day I swore I'd try to set things right." Damn, boy! You're on *fire!* Hot-*cha!* I have to remember this shit for when I retire with the 650K. Sit down there in Cancún and write a police novel. Bank robbery loot, that was one thing. But write a cop novel? Being a retired Philly cop with some scandal behind him? That was like printing money.

Saugherty looked down.

Lennon was holding the photo of his dead sister, naked and smeared with peanut butter.

But he didn't look down. He was studying Saugherty. Probably trying to figure how much of this was bullshit.

About ninety-nine percent, buddy, Saugherty thought.

Confessions of a Bank Robber

DEEP DOWN, LENNON KNEW HE COULDN'T TRUST Saugherty. And here he was, telling some story about crooked cops and helping people. Please. Who the fuck did this guy think he was talking to?

But since the guy was in a soul-baring mood, maybe it was time to play along.

At the very least it would be a way to get out of this hotel room. Back into the city proper. Find Katie, shoot everything that moved, then light out of Philadelphia forever.

Lennon pushed the police reports back on the desk and . . .

[Slight Return]

THANK YOU OH MY GENTLE JESUS HOLY FUCKING SHIT

Confessions [Cont'd]

. . . MADE THE BY-NOW FAMILIAR PANTOMIME. PEN. PAPER. Bring them to me.

Saugherty was a quick study. And he seemed awfully relieved that Lennon wasn't flipping through his precious case files any longer. Probably enough police corruption in there to make a hundred investigative journalists cream their pants. Who cared? Not Lennon.

They made an odd-looking pair at the front desk: Lennon, with his beat-up face and white hip-hop tracksuit; Saugherty, with his high-school-math-teacher sport coat and wrinkled-beyond-redemption button-down shirt. Saugherty looked like a suburban dad with a nasty secret. The age difference was about right. Lennon looked like he enjoyed it rough. Whatever.

The request for the key to the hotel's word-processing center seemed to take the clerk by surprise. Probably thought they wanted to surf for man-on-boy porn.

Again: whatever.

Once they were in the room and the busted-up looking Dell had booted up, Lennon started typing furiously. He'd learned to type by e-mailing Katie. It was the ideal way to communicate whenever work separated them, which was often. Granted, Lennon wasn't going to win any typing awards. He used two fingers in a modified hunt-and-peck fashion, occasionally bringing the thumb and middle fingers into play.

Saugherty read over his shoulder. "Ah. Yeah. That I know. Wachovia."

Lennon shot him a look.

"Sorry. Go ahead. Do your thing."

So Lennon continued his rundown of the weekend, from the heist itself to getting arrested this morning. It wasn't an emotional account. Pure business. Because that was what Saugherty wanted to hear, right? About the money. Because he knew that Saugherty just wanted Lennon to lead him to the money, at which point he'd be arrested or killed. Nothing had changed since Friday night. Actually, in a long weekend of turnabouts and backstabs, Saugherty's consistency was refreshing.

"No kidding! Shit, your own partner? That son of a bitch."

More typing.

"Yeah, the Russians. No surprise there. But how did the wops get involved—"

More typing.

"Ah. Gotcha. Which is why I got the shit kicked out of me

when I followed you down to that restaurant. Somehow, knowledge diminishes the pain, don't you think? Guy walks up to you out of nowhere, pops you in the kisser, you think, What the fuck? The question hurts just as bad as the punch. But say you find you were giving his baby sister the ol' sloppy push from behind. Now it makes sense all of a sudden. Am I right?"

Lennon ignored him and continued typing. He wished the ex-cop would shut the fuck up and pay attention to what he was writing.

More commentary:

"Unfuckingbelievable."

And:

"A cop—right there at the party?"

On and on.

The other reason Lennon was spilling his guts? He needed Saugherty's help figuring out this shit. Where *was* the money? Maybe there was still a spark of a keen analytical mind somewhere in that ex-cop's booze-addled brain. Maybe Saugherty could spot something Lennon had overlooked.

When Lennon finished, Saugherty let out one long whistle.

"Man. I almost feel bad shooting you in the shoulder and strapping you to a table. You've had one hell of a weekend, haven't you boss?"

Lennon typed:

help me rescue my sister. we find the money, split it . . . deal?

"Nah. We look for the money first."

NO TIME

Lennon stood up from the chair. He had options. Saugherty might have a gun, but it'd be tough to use in such close quarters. Lennon could hurl him through the plate-glass window that separated the word-processing center from the hotel lobby.

"Alright, alright. I'm not a prick. You want your sister safe. I'd want the same thing. And I know where she is; she's going to be fine. These are wannabe Mafiosi. I know 'em. They're lazy and greedy. They're not going to jeopardize their meal ticket. But here's the thing: we're on a deadline for the money, too. So consider this counterproposal."

Lennon nodded. *Go on.*

"Seems to me there's only one option with the money. Your third partner—this Crosby guy. You haven't seen him since the morning of the heist. You assume he's down that pipe, but you don't know.

"What you do know is that your other partner—the one who double-crossed you—doesn't have the money. 'Cause he'd be sitting back with his feet up in Cancún about now, sipping a Mai Tai and getting himself an Oriental massage complete with a happy ending. Am I right? So Crosby is the missing link."

Which is what Katie had said.

"So first we go to the pipe over in Camden and fish out the bodies. We find Crosby, fine. We got to look somewhere else. We don't find him, though, he's our guy. Then we get your sister and plan our next move. Deal?"

In the Bag

THE IRISH BASTARD NODDED. DEAL. SAUGHERTY smiled.

Of course, we're probably not going to find your pal Crosby, so I'll put you in that pipe in his place. Then I'll go after him. The heister with the money. Sorry Katie—you're beyond saving, sweetheart.

He watched Lennon quit Word and click the "Don't Save" box. His weekend memoir disappeared.

Then he looked at Saugherty and made a pistol with his right hand.

"Yes. Guns. We're going to need guns to get Katie, aren't we? Well, brother, you just happened upon the right retired cop. Come on back to the room. Got a surprise for you."

Not the faxed photo of dead Katie—Saugherty had already swiped it, folded it, and put it in his jacket pocket. No second mistakes.

The surprise was inside a green army duffel bag, the payoff for a favor he had done a Philly S.W.A.T. team member some years ago—covering up a wife-beating beef. In return, Saugherty had asked for a bag of tricks: heavy artillery stuff he could keep off the books. The bag certainly came in handy from time to time. This time being one of them.

Saugherty thought he'd be using this stuff in a standoff with some of his former colleagues, if it came to that. It was part of his exit strategy. But now it was looking like he had another option, after all.

"Isn't this sweet?"

Lennon didn't seem impressed. He chose two .38s, and it was

obvious he didn't know much about guns, as he didn't do much in the way of shopping. He was like an amateur home owner grabbing the first available tool to stop the leaky kitchen faucet. Didn't matter if it was a hammer or pliers or a screwdriver or a chainsaw.

Saugherty, on the other hand, chose carefully. He skipped the pistols and rifles. He wasn't going to need them. Instead, he dipped into special ordinance: an oversized flare-gun-looking thing. It held two flashbang grenades, used by S.W.A.T. teams to disorient and confuse their targets. The sonic blast was enough to render ten men unconscious at close range. Eardrums would be burst. Nasal vessels would rupture. Eyes would bleed.

The bank robber was giving him a quizzical look.

"What? This? Flare gun. It's a distraction. For when we go after your sister. This'll confuse the hell out of the wops."

That seemed to satisfy Lennon, who checked his pistols to make sure they were loaded. Of course they were. All part of the exit strategy.

And the other part was this: once they determined that Crosby was a no-show at his own funeral, Saugherty would dump a flashbang grenade in Lennon's lap. That might be enough to kill him, but probably not. Either way, he'd dump him and the pistol down the pipe, then hightail it out of there.

Track down Crosby. Squeeze him. Retire.

"Ready to go, brother?"

MONDAY
P.M. [LATER]

Tell the boys I'm coming home.

— WILBUR UNDERHILL

Flash
Bang
Bang
Bang

WHAT IMPRESSED LENNON MOST, THINKING BACK ON it, was how everything seemed blurred—dreamlike yet harried—after they left the hotel. Earlier in the day, the drive to the Northeast had taken forever. Now, I-95 was all but empty and they rocketed down the length of the Delaware River and crossed the Ben Franklin Bridge (yeah, again) to the Camden side within minutes. It was more like experiencing a fevered deathbed flashback than actual life.

Then they pulled up to a concrete parking pad within view of the pipes. And it got even worse.

Lennon couldn't believe what he was seeing.

There were three people down there carrying two body bags toward the pipe. At first, Lennon thought he was watching a replay of his own near-burial from Friday night. But no, these were three different people, carrying—presumably—two different corpses to the mouth of the pipe. The one that was due to be covered with a thick slab of concrete in the near future.

Saugherty saw them, too. "What is this? A Mafia fire sale? Bury all of your dead now while prices stay rock-bottom? Who the fuck are these guys?"

Lennon squinted. He made one of them out.

Big guy. Pasty. Tortoiseshell glasses. Ugly moustache.

It was the guy from the South Philly basement. And his buddies. The ones who had held a gun to Katie's head.

The body bag.

Plastic.

Sized just right.

Katie.

The blurring stopped. Everything seemed clear now.

Lennon turned, pointed one of the .38s at Saugherty's armpit—not covered by Kevlar—then pulled the trigger.

The ex-cop had been distracted by the strangers. "What . . . ?" Then, upon looking down. "I . . . can't fucking believe this." A dark damp stain spread down across the sleeve of his shirt.

Lennon left the car and made his way down to the pipes. He heard the driver's door creak open behind him. Saugherty was trying to crawl out. Let him. He'd finish him later.

The gunshot hadn't alarmed the three guys down below. After all, this was Camden. But the creaking door was another story.

They all looked up in Lennon's direction.

By this point, Lennon was racing toward them, a gun in each hand. He had only two thoughts. First: see Katie with my own eyes. Then: exterminate. The rest would fall into place.

"What the fuck?" said one of them.

"Hey, it's him," said the big guy with the tortoiseshell glasses. "The bank robber."

Lennon shot him right between the lenses.

His two pals dropped the body bag and reached for their weapons, but Lennon stopped and aimed a pistol at each of them and shook his head. *No.*

This wasn't the deterrent that Lennon hoped it would be. They drew their guns anyway. Pointed them at Lennon.

"He wants you to open those bags," said a voice.

It was Saugherty, that crazy bastard. Staggering toward them with that oversized flare gun in his hand.

"Frankly, I'm just as curious as he is. So why don't you do us all a favor and unzip 'em?"

The two henchmen, who looked like twins now that Lennon had a chance to think about it, appeared puzzled. But not for long.

Gunfire snapped to life everywhere.

"Oh, fuck me up the ass!"

Bullets sparked off the concrete slab, and ripped through fabric and flesh.

"Shit! Shit!"

Then came a *phhhh-WOOM* sound.

In the microsecond it took for Lennon to lose consciousness, he came to realize: Yes, this was it.

This was the death flashback.

All of it.

Pure

White

THOSE S.W.A.T. GUYS DON'T DICK AROUND, SAUGHERTY thought, as the smoking flashbang grenade pistol twirled once and slipped out of his hand. It didn't have far to fall. Saugherty was already flat on his back on the concrete floor.

He sniffed blood, briefly noted that his eyes felt like burning charcoal briquettes, then passed out.

But not before he had one more thought: Shit, I'd hate to see the other guy.

Here Comes the Groom

5 SAUGHERTY WOKE UP SOME TIME LATER. IMMEDIATELY, he knew that someone else had beat him to consciousness.

He could hear him moving around.

The best idea right now: play dead. Which wasn't difficult, considering he had a bullet swimming around his armpit somewhere, and he was partially numb. Then, look for an opening. Take it. Just like he always did. Saugherty could imagine that sentiment etched on his tombstone.

Saugherty was used to playing dead and stealing peeks. He used to do it when he was eight years old, during sleepovers at his cousins' house. His teenaged female cousins. The ones who slept only in panties. And who often grew thirsty in the middle of the night and bounced off for a cold glass of Delaware Punch. God, Saugherty missed those sleepovers.

But here, now, something bugged him. He'd blasted that flashbang grenade right in the middle of the three of them: Lennon, and his two Italian pals. If he wasn't mistaken, the grenade actually nailed one of the wops right in the balls. No way *he* was up and about—checking bodies, smoking cigarettes, ordering pizza. Probably not his twin brother, either. Could be Lennon, but that didn't make sense either. Saugherty had been standing a good ten yards behind Lennon. If Saugherty had been knocked out, Lennon's head should have been knocked off.

He took a chance.

He peeked.

Nope. There was Lennon, sprawled on the concrete in what appeared to be a supremely uncomfortable position. Even for Tantric sex.

Which meant . . . ?

A rough hand slapped him across the face. Saugherty's eyes popped open.

"Hey there."

The guy looking down at him . . . now this was a new character entirely. Saugherty tried spinning through his mental Rolodex but came up with a big goose egg.

"Who are you?"

"Michael Kowalski," the guy said. He was thin yet muscular, with slightly beady eyes and razor-sharp black hair in a crew cut. He was wearing all black—even the gun rig strapped to his chest. "And you?"

"Saugherty. I'm an ex-cop."

Then, playing a hunch:

"You look like you're on the job, too."

"I am. Sort of."

"FBI?"

"Used to be. Bank robbery squad."

"And now?"

"Something else."

"CIA?"

"Something like that. It's a department they don't talk about much on the evening news." Michael scanned the area around the pipe. "There are a lot of dead bodies. Some are already pre-bagged. What happened here, Saugherty?"

All of them dead? Including Lennon? Saugherty felt the white heat of hope burn in his stomach. It even eased the pain from the bullet.

"Guy in the white tracksuit is a bank robber. Did the Wachovia job on Friday. I've been pursuing him freelance. At the request of the mayor himself."

Yeah, that sounded good. Even started out being true. In a way.

"The mayor? Really?"

"Yeah. Check with . . . well, Lt. Mothers is dead. But check with his replacement. You'll see."

Michael considered this.

"Are you sure the guy in the white suit is dead?" asked Saugherty. "He's one tough fucker."

"I checked for a pulse. Not much going on there. If he's not dead yet, it's a matter of minutes. So . . . wait a second. I can't keep calling you Saugherty. That makes it sound like we're in a bad TV cop movie. What's your first name?"

A pause. "Harold."

"Harry, is it?"

"No. Harold. That's why it's 'Saugherty.'" He coughed up something wet. "Ah, shit, don't make me laugh."

"Harold, who are these other guys? They don't look like bank robbers to me."

"Some mobsters, I'm guessing. This bank robber, Patrick Selway Lennon, had a money-laundering deal with them." Wow. That was good. Keep spinning, keep spinning. "There was even talk that they did the scouting for the Wachovia job. A pure moneymaker. They're basically a bunch of washed-up losers trying to get back in the game."

"Interesting," Michael said, then walked over to the dead twins. Or what looked like the remnants of the dead twins.

Sirens wailed in the distance.

"Those your guys?" Saugherty asked.

"Nah. My guy's over there."

"Who?" Oh no. What was this? Was he one of Perelli's guys?

"The bank robber in the white tracksuit. He was my brother-in-law. Or was going to be, anyway."

Even though he was numb, Saugherty could feel the icy-blast effect of a cold fusion bomb in his stomach.

"Which brings me to my next question, Harold."

"Yeah?"

"Why is there a photograph of my dead fiancée in your jacket pocket?"

Saugherty didn't have an answer for that one.

So Michael Kowalski picked him up and threw him down the pipe.

Family

KOWALSKI CLEANED UP AS FAST AS HE COULD—YEP, there were sirens approaching. And no cover would be adequate to explain his presence in the middle of a Camden, New Jersey, bloodbath. Not even his government creds. So his valediction would have to be on the short side.

He rolled his dead brother-in-law-to-be over on his back.

"Nice to finally meet you, Pat," Michael said.

Lennon stared up blankly. Dark blood had leaked from his tear ducts, nostrils, and ears—as if his brain were a tomato and someone had squished it.

"This is not how I imagined our first meeting. I was looking forward to our time in Puerto Rico. A little baccarat, some steaks, some rum. Not this.

"Well, perhaps *this*. Eventually. A brother-in-law on the Ten Most Wanted list can be a liability to a guy in my profession, you know? But to be honest, I hadn't made up my mind about you yet.

Katie was so in love with you—she idolized you. I didn't see how you could possibly live up to your reputation.

"And now that I see you, and now that I've seen my dead fiancée and unborn child on a slab in a police morgue . . . well, I've gotta say. I'm disappointed. Did you even know her? Did you know she'd do anything for you?

"Ah, maybe I'm being harsh. I don't even know you. Maybe you tried your best.

"Maybe you didn't.

"Maybe I'm going to have to finish what you started here tonight."

Michael stared down at Lennon and, after some consideration, made the sign of the cross. The sirens were almost upon him.

"Okay, good talk, bro."

Michael picked up Lennon, then carried him over to the pipe.

Lennon floated across the blood-splattered concrete slab, his lifeless body headed toward the pipe.

Had he been a smoker, Lennon would have savored a last few puffs before smashing the butt into the metal lip of the pipe. Just one cigarette—something for the geeks in khaki pants and navy blue windbreakers to pick up with tweezers, drop into a thick Ziploc bag, tag, log, then store in their evidence cases.

Maybe someone would have gotten around to analyzing the brand, try to pluck some DNA from the butt.

Maybe some part of Lennon would have lived forever.

a
Beautiful
Friendship

OH, IT WAS BAD. SAUGHERTY DIDN'T HAVE ANY ILLU-
sions. The wound under his right arm was pumping blood
like a kid's water pistol. The impact of sliding down the pipe had
snapped his spine, and he couldn't feel his fingers anymore. He was
folded like a V inside a dank, fetid, slimy, and circular metal coffin.
There were soft, squishy things beneath him. Bodies. He had been
to enough crime scenes to distinguish the degrees of ripeness.

But at least he wasn't upside down. Saughtery could look up
and see the night sky through the opening of the pipe.

Things were looking up already, he thought to himself, and
chuckled, which hurt.

Then a hand appeared in the opening, and an arm. Draping itself over the side.

A head, in shadow.

What the hell . . . ?

The opening of the pipe suddenly went dark. Saugherty heard
a scraping sound that became louder and louder until—

Impact. A hard skull pounded into his chest. An elbow
smashed his nose, and another slammed into the middle of his
left shin.

That Michael asshole had pitched his own brother-in-law—
well, his almost brother-in-law—into the pipe.

Which made no fucking sense whatsoever.

"You son of a bitch," Saugherty finally mumbled, when the
waves of shock and pain finally ebbed. He took his frustrations out
on Lennon's body. "Shouldn't you be out collecting your money?
Isn't that what this is all about?"

Nothing.

"I know you're still alive. I can feel your body breathing."

Nothing.

"You're trembling. You're scared, ain't ya?"

Still nothing.

"Goddamnit, I wish you could have held on to your voice a bit longer. 'Cause you know, I'm really dying to know what was going through your head the past couple of days."

Saugherty felt the trembling increase. At first, he thought the mute bank robber was going through death spasms. His body finally giving out. After a while, he realized he was wrong.

Lennon was *laughing*.

NEWS BULLETS

Cement foundation poured for New Jersey's children's museum

After countless political delays and bitter turf squabbles, the new Children's Discovery Museum in Camden, NJ, took one step closer to reality as workers laid the museum's thick concrete foundation. "The first kids will be running through the front doors in about seven months," promised wunderkind developer Jeffrey Greenblatt. "This will breathe new life into the dead urban center that is Camden."

13th dead Perelli associate . . . linked to mystery slayer?

The mob wars in Philadelphia continue to heat up this summer, even though members from both the Perelli and Barone families deny they're feuding. The latest victim: 45-year-old Manny Namako, a suspected arsonist and bookmaker, found dead in the bathroom of his South Philly row home. "The police need to investigate this for what it is: a madman with a rifle preying on innocent businessmen," mob lawyer Dan Behuniak told reporters yesterday.

Officially, police refuse to acknowledge the rumors that a vigilante dubbed "Mr. K" has been systematically erasing alleged wise guys for the past nine weeks.

But one law-enforcement insider confirms: "Yeah, there's somebody out there. He's pissed. And he's a good shot, too."

Strange odor disturbs summer visitors to NJ kids' museum

"Like old fish and cheese . . . ick!" says Alison Eaton, 10, of her July visit to the Children's Discovery Museum.

Kids are discovering things, all right. They're discovering how adept their noses are at detecting foul odors.

For some unexplained reason, the brand-new museum is inundated with an odor that one security guard—a Vietnam War veteran—could only compare it to "the stench of bloated bodies floating along the Mekong Delta."

"We have the best environmental forensic analysts in the country working on it," responds Jeffrey Greenblatt, the young, troubled developer who has watched multiple projects fizzle at the last moment. This, however, could spell the breaking point for Greenblatt, real-estate analysts say, as well as the end of new development in Philadelphia or Camden for years to come.

$100 from Wachovia heist recovered

LAS VEGAS, NV.—Police made an arrest today in the months-old Wachovia bank heist after a Philly resident used a hundred dollar bill to pay for beer and pornography magazines in a convenience store.

Dylan McManus, 20, aroused the suspicions of the clerk when he insisted he was a "high roller from Philadelphia" and didn't need to be carrying I.D. for beer. The clerk took the bill, then called the FBI, who traced McManus to a motel in Laughlin.

Previously, McManus had been employed as a security guard at Park-o-Matic, a park-it-yourself lot based in downtown Philadelphia.

Special Thanks to . . .

Sunshine, for debuting it.
The Pope, for inspiring it.
Tenacious DHS, for pimping it.
Marc, for buying it, editing it, vastly improving it.
Marsha, for believing in it.
Father Luke, for blessing it.
Meredith, Parker, and **Sarah,** without whom there would be no "it."

And to My Heist Crew: John Cunningham, Becki Heller, Jessie Hutcheson, and the rest of Team Minotaur. J.T., K-Buster, Kafka, and the PointBlankers. Mark "the Man" Stanton. Simon Hynd and Micky MacPherson. Gary the Hat. Loren Feldman. Jason Schwartz. Rich Rys. Paul, Hickey, B.H., Lori and my co-workers at the *CP*. Mike "Rego" Regan. Tony Fiorentino. Deacon Clark. Mr. Aleas. Mr. Keene. Mr. Starr. The Other Mr. Smith (Anthony Neil). The Gischler. La Salle University. Wachovia Bank. And to all of my friends and family.

about the author

DUANE SWIERCZYNSKI IS EDITOR-IN-CHIEF OF THE *Philadelphia City Paper.* A receipt for *This Here's a Stick-Up,* Duane's nonfiction book on American bank robbery, was found in the getaway car of a San Francisco bandit who'd hit at least thirty California banks. Duane lives in Philadelphia. Visit his Web site at www.duaneswierczynski.com.